Kalila

For Lesley,
— in a shared
love of words

Best
Rosemary
x

Other books by Rosemary Nixon

The Cock's Egg
Mostly Country: Stories

Kalila

ROSEMARY NIXON

GOOSE LANE

Edited by Bethany Gibson.
Cover image detailed from an image by sskies, morguefile.com.
Cover and page design by Julie Scriver.
Printed in Canada.
10 9 8 7 6 5 4 3 2 1

Library and Archives Canada Cataloguing in Publication

Nixon, Rosemary, 1952-
Kalila / Rosemary Nixon.

ISBN 978-0-86492-652-4

I. Title.
PS8577.I95K35 2011   C813'.54   C2010-907057-7

Also issued in electronic form under ISBN 978-0-86492-699-9

Goose Lane Editions acknowledges the financial support of the Canada Council for the Arts, the Government of Canada through the Book Publishing Industry Development Program (BPIDP), and the New Brunswick Department of Wellness, Culture, and Sport for its publishing activities.

Goose Lane Editions
Suite 330, 500 Beaverbrook Court
Fredericton, New Brunswick
CANADA E3B 5X4
www.gooselane.com

For Kiala

$$\frac{\partial H}{\partial p_i} , \qquad \dot{p}_i = -\frac{\partial H}{\partial q_i}$$

π is poisson bracket of two variables

$$[u, v] = \sum_k \left[\frac{\partial u}{\partial q_k} \frac{\partial v}{\partial p_k} - \frac{\partial u}{\partial p_k} \frac{\partial v}{\partial q_k} \right]$$

one

Then $\dfrac{du}{dt} = [u, H] + \dfrac{\partial u}{\partial t}$

Then $\dfrac{du}{dt} = [u, H] + \dfrac{\partial u}{\partial t}$

Quantum

$\nabla \cdot B = 0 \qquad \nabla \times \vec{E} + \dfrac{1}{c} \dfrac{\partial \vec{B}}{\partial t} = 0$

$\nabla \cdot \vec{D} = 4\pi \rho \qquad \nabla \times \vec{H} - \dfrac{1}{c} \dfrac{\partial \vec{D}}{\partial t} = \dfrac{4\pi}{c} \vec{J}$

where $\vec{E} =$ electric field, $\vec{B} =$ magnetic field

and $\vec{D} = \vec{E} + 4\pi \vec{P} ; \qquad \vec{H} = \vec{B} - 4\pi \vec{M}$

$\nabla \cdot \vec{B} = 0 \qquad \nabla \times \vec{E} + \dfrac{1}{c} \dfrac{\partial \vec{B}}{\partial t} = 0$

$\nabla \cdot \vec{E} = 0 \qquad \nabla \times \vec{B} - \dfrac{1}{c} \dfrac{\partial \vec{E}}{\partial t} = 0$

$\nabla^2 \vec{E} - \dfrac{1}{c^2} \dfrac{\partial^2 \vec{E}}{\partial t^2}$

$\vec{E} = \vec{E}_0 e$

Brodie

The news is like staring into an eclipse of the sun. Look at it straight and you'll go blind.

You prepared. You prepared for a child to be born. You have not prepared for this. You stand at the window of your classroom and look out past your plants. You can see down to the smoking door. Kids huddled in bunches without their coats. Their breath rising, cloudy spirals.

Roses. You must bring Maggie roses. For a moment, shifting through papers on your desk, hunting the missing wire for tomorrow's torsion bar experiment, you forget. Forget you have a baby. This baby. You take a breath and bend into your chair. Your students sit quiet in their desks. Some are looking at you; others look away. You say, When a wave passes from deep water into shallow, the ray refracts toward the normal. You want to say, Today is cancelled. You think the baby's name. *Kalila. Beloved.* The students go about their work, filling water tables, generating waves.

When water rolls from deep to shallow, you say, it can create a tidal wave.

Miraculously, the day ends.

You pack your satchel with student lab reports, drive to a florist. Ask for a dozen roses. The young woman behind the counter winks, says, Well, have we got hopes tonight! Gets glum when you don't answer.

At the hospital, you step off on the fifth floor, Neonatal Intensive Care. And wonder how you got here.

Maggie

I sit in Neonatal ICU and imagine a daughter. Fluorescent lights stare down, a worker vacuums. Ninety machines hum. Our baby. This girl. The baby next to Kalila's isolette was born last night without a brain. His eyes stare out. There's nothing in there. I have to look away. The mother sits beside his isolette, unmoving. Iceberg face. It pulses through me. Sudden choking laughter. *You look just like your baby.* I look down at mine, eyes closed, legs splayed, blue diaper dwarfing her. Inside burning. She will be reckless, this daughter, Kalila. She will play hard, be a tomboy, scrape shins, throw a football, throw herself into her history.

Throw away this picture, Maggie.

An acquaintance, Judith, is sitting on a bench in the waiting room. I hardly know her. The husband left her two, three months ago. I see the woman on occasion, at the grocery store, at church. We never talk. This morning Judith shows up at the hospital. Dark coat, rubber boots, no earrings.

You can't get in, I tell her. They barely allow family. You can't stay. Even my sisters have trouble getting in.

Two hours now. There she sits, on a hard bench in the waiting room. Offering no words.

I look over at the iceberg mother.

Dr. Norton enters the nursery. The one doctor who never dresses like a doctor. Today she's wearing a floral-print skirt. It shows beneath her lab coat. Dr. Norton carries a chart, moves to the isolette next to Kalila's. Her sleeve touches that mother cast in ice.

Good morning, Mrs. Angonata. The woman doesn't answer. The doctor pulls up a stool, sits down beside her. Expels a breath. There's not a lot we can do for your son. He's being kept warm and safe.

A twitch. The woman shakes. She shimmers in this cold, blue-lit neonatal nursery.

We don't know how long. Some hours? Perhaps several days. No, you don't have to hold him. No, some mothers choose not to. Please, call me any time. Wait, no, it's not too hard. It's just the cords get caught. I'll help you lift him out. She lifts the empty baby, empty dangling legs, stare fixed on nothing. Lifts him from the mess of wires into a frozen mother's arms.

Mother. Doctor. Judith on a hard bench. Maggie Rachael Watson.

Under fluorescent lights, four women without a language stare into the present.

Dr. Vanioc

Dr. W. P. Vanioc rubs his neck, picks up a pen, and reads.

October 17
Operation Report Progress Notes
524010
Solantz Girl
Problem List:
1. Respiratory distress
2. Dysmorphic features
3. Auditory evoked responses show abnormal
4. Solantz, girl, has decreased calcium and
   magnesium
5. Was put on digoxin 0.1 mg p.o. bid, followed by
   Dr. Showalter
6. Solantz, girl, kept on 38% oxygen.
7. Goes off colour during feeds.

Dr. Vanioc unties his shoelaces, leans back in his chair, raises his arms to ease his headache, and returns to the child's chart.

The baby came in a week ago, transferred from the Peter Lougheed Centre on her third day. She has everything wrong with her, and no reason that he can see. Slightly under four weeks early. Normal delivery, although they induced the mother due to toxemia. The right side of the child's mouth shows evidence of facial paralysis. She has excessive mucus secretions from her nose and throat. Her feedings result in coughing and choking and vomiting. She already has developed upper-lobe aspiration pneumonia as a result. The ductus is still open. The babe's on 40% oxygen. Dr. Vanioc makes notes on his pad. He will suggest Lasix, put her on digoxin. He reviews the nurses' reports.

Neonatal Intensive Care Flow Sheet
Oct. 11: 4:30 p.m.:

Babe received on 50% oxygen. Colour dusky.
Passed large sticky meconium. Appears jaundiced.
Coffee-ground-like material in white mucus. Not
tolerating oral feeds. IV restarted in scalp vein.
Babe dusky and apneac. Respiration shallow.
Jittery when disturbed. Two bradys.

Parents in to visit. Apprehensive.

The doctor twists his wedding band around his finger. His headache makes him want to take it off. The babe developed hypocalcemia and was given an IV of calcium gluconate. Feedings started again twelve hours ago. The infant sucks moderately well, but her pulmonary signs are worsening. Likely more aspiration. The parents young, but not so young. Late twenties maybe. The mother exhibits high anxiety. She's small and worried, like a wired spring.

Dr. Vanioc takes off his glasses, rubs his eyes. He thinks of his wife, at this moment spooning mushed peas and puréed squash into his small son's mouth, irritated that her husband gives sixteen hours a day to these sick babies while he neglects his own. Dr. Vanioc thinks of his wife's indignant back, the fine curve of her spine where it reaches her buttocks, thinks this for a moment, then pushes it into the headache that climbs his neck. He turns back to the charts.

Möbius syndrome? he scribbles.

They'll have to feed her through gastrostomy.

Brodie

The angled doors of Foothills Hospital slide apart, and you enter the smells — floor polish, coffee, corned beef, flowers, medication, pus. You think, We exist because of an explosion of stars. O_2, CO_2, H_2. You got the mail before you drove here. Maggie's mother sent a baby quilt, bits from her Saskatchewan sewing sunroom, a starburst pattern, tiny triangles of brown, blue, green, yellow, patterned, cotton, linen, gabardine, hand-stitched leftovers from Maggie's childhood.

The elevator pings. A group of anxious visitors herds on and mills while everybody stabs a button. This morning you explained Schrödinger's cat experiment to your grade eleven class. A box, an unfortunate cat shoved in a box, radioactive material, and a potentially lethal device. This device could kill the cat, depending on whether the radioactive pellet emits a particle and triggers the device. There is a 50-50 chance. You step out of the elevator and head down the hall. The observer's paradox. The scientists outside the closed box have no idea of the fate of the cat, which remains in a state of superposition, of limbo: the cat alive *and* dead, or neither alive *nor* dead — until an observer opens the box and looks inside. You scrub your hands, don the yellow gown, open the heavy door, and step into the cold, sharp neonatal climate. Breathe its absence: a stroller ride, a winter toque, tugs on a mother's nipple, a rubber ball. A series of bleating beeps. A nurse calls, Brady. Baby Heisler. Got it.

You look at the sweeping reach of babies, bereft of the smell of oranges, autumn quilts, iced tea. A room full of babies who cannot see the stars. You wind to your baby's isolette and peer down at the child breathing in great gulps, as if the air were uncertain, retreating from her. Einstein never accepted Schrödinger's quantum mechanics. Einstein said God doesn't play dice with the world. You reach into the child's isolette, rub your thumb, like rubbing Aladdin's lamp, against the baby's forehead and an agonizing flush of hope bursts across your skin. You straighten the cords, arrange the files flung atop her isolette, collect two pens, some lint, a piece of napkin from the floor.

Order in the world.

Maggie

Foothills Neonatal ICU breathes story. Stories weave the isolettes, the suction machines, heart monitors, the oxygen tubes, the heaving ventilators. They cling to the hems of nursing uniforms and ride the lapels of doctors' lab coats. They smell, these stories, these angry prayers.

I hold Kalila on my lap, an intravenous needle stuck in her head. Yellow bruises criss-cross her shaved scalp where intravenous needles went interstitial. Even needles fail my baby. When I was a child, farmboys caught frogs, cut off their legs, and let them go. The frenetic gyrate of legs, the bulging eyes. Stop it! I hate you! Sobbing. The boys laughing.

Just being boys.

Kalila fights like that when the nurses suction her. Her fists punch out, head wheels from side to side. I conserve strength for those suction episodes — twelve, fifteen times a day. A tube inserted up the baby's nose, tiny mouth open in a gag, push farther, farther, frog legs jerking, a nurse hauling tubing like a hose snaked down a drain hole. White-green gunk sucking up the hose, spastic limbs, the baby's face a caricature of anguish. The nurses step around me, doing their job.

Dr. Staszick enters. One of the boys. The head nurse is also one of the boys. This is an old boys' club and we have crashed it. Nobody likes us here. Nobody likes my baby. I ask permission to bathe Kalila. To lift her into a warm water basin. The surprise of skin on skin. Baby, you exist. We're really touching. I know to arrange the gastrostomy tube inserted in the baby's stomach, to keep hold of it twelve centimetres down the tube so gravity won't pressure and pull it free, to arrange the oxygen tube, the heart monitor attachment tubes, her intravenous lines. My fingers support her at the small of her neck. Kalila finds herself in water, her expression is surprise. I lap water against her belly, the soles of her feet. Cheek against my baby's head until her features lose their tenseness, her head moves to touch her cheek to mine and she kicks. For one strange moment the institution smell lifts, and I am a live whole mom holding a live whole baby.

No bath! Nurse says no time this morning. Beepers are going off. Babies are trying to die. The nurse has filled a basin with water, then abandons it when the baby next to Kalila goes into cardiac arrest. The nurse moves fast, her elbow catches the baby's foot, which hits the basin, knocks it to the floor, and now the cleaning staff has been called in — more bodies, more equipment.

I hum. It's an act of rebellion. I hum to Kalila, who ignores her bathwater sweeping the neonatal floor.

My baby's life here at Foothills Hospital is one big awful song. *Ninety-nine bottles of beer on the wall. Ninety-nine bottles of beer.* Fragments. Bleak and rhythmic. The sickening repetitive pattern. *Pass one down. Hand it around.* Same tune, same words. Fewer bottles.

Brodie

The lab benches are cluttered with archaic meters and ring stands and retort stands. The pipes bang, someone has turned the water on upstairs. Dan Lemer is making origami from his physics handout sheet.

Okay, class. A quick review. Who did the first experiments on light? you ask your grade elevens.

Isaac Newton, Mr. Solantz.

Good, Malik. When?

Sometime in the 1600s.

It appears to be a miniature piano.

Tell us how Newton did it. You knock your knuckles on a desk. Pearl straightens sharply. Dan abandons the piano and starts in on a swan. You take great breaths. Breathe air breathed by kids who care about basketball and scoring. Kids whose expectations for you are not to fix them, just to pass on information.

What instigated the experiment?

A sunbeam shining through a crack in a blind, sir.

You betcha. Gavin, do your chemistry homework in chemistry class. This is physics. He let it fall at an angle on a triangular glass prism and set up a white screen the beam would strike against. The beam was already bent upon entering, and of course it was bent much farther when it came out the prism on the other side. To his surprise, he found — what did he find?

A bunch of colours.

Right, Lazar. Instead of forming a white light, the sunbeam spread itself into a band of colours. To which, by the way, Newton added indigo, though no one knew exactly what colour indigo was. Some say he named it after his niece, others a lover. Newton wasn't always bright — he did get sun-blindness from his experiments.

I heard Newton was gay! pipes Gaganpreet from the back.

Indigo is not gender-specific, Gaganpreet. For some reason Newton wanted seven. Seven was magical, the influence of alchemy. The notion exists — you scratch out a layered pictogram on the worn blackboard in this archaic room, in Calgary's oldest school — that butterfly wings are layers of transparent scales. Like so? Each species layers in a unique arrangement. This means, of course, butterflies refract light in different wavelengths, hence they appear — ?

— as different colours.

Dan's hand has been waving through your entire talk.

Hey, Mr. Solantz, you spelled *spectrum* wrong.

Jesus, fix it in your book, says Huong.

Good solution, Huong. More influence from you and we'll have Daniel here thinking on his own. You slap the chalk dust off your hands. Feel almost happy. It hovers in the morning light. We rarely think about light, or the eyes we see it with. Did you know, grade elevens, that you see some things better by looking sideways? In good light you see clearly and in colour, right? But take something that gives off only a faint light, such as a small night star, you'll actually see it only if you look *beside* it —

Cool. Dan has turned in his desk, grinning flirtatiously at Huong.

— causing the light to fall on our retina where our rods, those bits of our eye that detect light, are closely bunched.

That's not where Dan's rod is, Huong mutters.

Dan calls, Hey, sir, I know what spectrum means in Latin. Ghost!

Who says dead languages aren't useful? you say. Yoohoo, anybody home, Oleg? Feet on the floor. It was Newton, as well, who first decided that light consisted of tiny particles travelling at tremendous speed. You drop your piece of chalk from hand to hand, weave among your students. But in 1678, pens ready? the Dutch physicist Christiaan Huygens found proof for an opposing theory. He believed that light consisted not of particles but of very tiny waves. This made sense to him because it explained the differing refraction of the different kinds of light. The shorter the wavelength, he thought, the greater the refraction. Which colour, by the way, has the shortest wavelength?

Red.

Nope. Gurpyar?

Violet.

Right. Which has the longest?

Red. I guess.

Good guess. Didn't your grade six teacher make you memorize Roy G. Biv? Red, orange, yellow, green, blue, indigo, violet?

The kids are staring at you with incredulity.

But Huygens's theory didn't answer everything. Discoveries, class, only serve to open up more mysteries. Why, for instance, light waves can't go around obstacles, though sound waves can.

The students' eyes are on the clock. Countdown to lunchtime. You lay aside your chalk. To this day, nobody knows for sure what light is. You perch on your desk, hope the day will never end. The students' shuffling quiets.

Try this. If you think you know what light is, set up an experiment — and you know what results you'll get? You'll get the results you want. If you think light is made up of photons or particles, you can arrange an experiment that will prove light behaves like tiny pellets shot from a gun. But hang on. Your lab mate sets up another experiment and proves that light acts like a pebble dropped into a creek — it circles out in waves. So what is light? Frankly, we don't know. Why don't we know? Because, grade elevens, each time we make an observation, we change the thing observed.

Uh-uh. You don't pack up until the bell rings. Alan, get your binder back out. Scientists have made countless discoveries with their experiments, but the smart ones use their imaginations. Dream possibility. What did Albert Einstein say? Imagination is more important than knowledge.

The classroom empties. Chalk dust down your pants.

Maggie

Three sculpted ivory heads sit on the woman's desk. Two clamp their eyes shut. The third stares at me; I stare back, clenching a booklet tossed on the oval coffee table: *Perinatal Bereavement. The Unique Nature and Factors Surrounding the Death or Acute Illness of a Child.* Footsteps squeak, the swish of nurses' uniforms, low rumble of food trolleys rolling wonky down the hall. Roast beef, well done. The social worker flips the pages of my file. I lean back against the brocade chair and consider the woman's outsized purse and burnt orange fingernails. Never thought to make a fashion statement when I dressed this morning. I consider my grass stained running shoes, consider the walls of this sterile office, forget-me-not blue. The flipping stops, the social worker caught on a page, like Skipper on point, eyes glued to a squirrel. Ah, yes. The woman's finger stabs against a word, the buttons on her suit jacket sleeve gleam gunmetal.

Let's start with this morning's situation, the social worker says.

The chair in which I have been deposited is designed for someone with metre-long thighs. Unless I slide forward, which leaves me leaning helplessly at a forty-five-degree angle, my running shoes sticking straight out from the knee.

This morning, in Neonatal ICU. The social worker taps her fingers against the desk, a cheerful clicking, and waits for me to take up the ball.

Are you sleeping well? she says. Because there are pills.

I wipe salty moisture from my hands. I had a dream, I say. My budgie, Dicky, I had him as a child, every night I said, Pretty bird, Dicky, pretty bird, pretty bird, before I covered his cage.

The social worker leans forward. So what was the dream?

That was it. Right there. I never owned a budgie. I am at his cage wearing rubber high-heeled shoes. I have a blanket in my hands, and I'm saying, Pretty bird, Dicky, pretty bird. Then I cover his cage. And I can't see him anymore.

The woman clears her throat. Shall we talk about this morning?

No.

Mrs. Solantz. The doctors, the nurses on fifth — the woman takes by the head the statue that has been staring me down and sternly rearranges it. One blue shoe dangles off her foot.

I'm Ms. Watson.

They're worried about you. You need to talk to someone.

I do talk. My husband. My sisters. I have friends. Milk sponge-leaks from my rock-hard breasts.

Your baby has been in the intensive care unit almost four weeks now?

Twenty-three days.

When have the doctors last spoken to you of her prognosis?

But I sit stony in my chair. Never again this morning's surprising sweep of sobs, the other mothers' panicked, averted faces, like I'd thrown up, soiled my underwear.

Don't blame yourself. The woman leans across her desk, pats my arm, an awkward, unfamiliar gesture. I hadn't known I should.

Here, grief is — the baby opens her blue-tinged mouth — emotional extremes all mixed — anxiety, anger, fear —

I breathe, huuuuuu. Breathe. Huuuuuu.

Oh, dear — perhaps this isn't the best — Let's bring you back when you feel more comfortable.

My body a river: mucus and blood and breast milk. The social worker, scrambling through her daybook.

A week from Friday — get yourself together — here, this tissue, no — of course we know it's hard.

Lady. You have no fucking idea.

Dr. Vanioc

Dr. Vanioc snaps a rubber band. He hasn't slept in days. Two nights on call, and last night, his son, teething, cried for hours.

He is mulling over the Solantz baby case. A scrawny child, somewhat wasted, though born at five pounds, unlike most of the babies who rarely make three, but she lost a pound initially and has made little gains to this point. He shifts through papers. The child continues to have dusky spells. The nurses' report indicates they had to leave the IV out this afternoon after four failed attempts to restart. The child's veins are collapsing. Tonight her temp's up.

The doctor makes a note. He'll add penicillin to the digoxin and Tri-Vi-Sol. She has copious amounts of thick, creamy secretions. Why can't the child swallow?

The latest chest X-ray shows bilateral upper-lobe atelectasis plus some consolidations. He taps the page. The electro-encephalogram shows some mildly slow generalized waves but within the range of normal. Her barium swallow revealed a grade four reflux and Maxeran was unsuccessful. The current thought among the doctors is that the child has a brain stem abnormality. That's possible, and yet—Dr. Vanioc removes his glasses, rubs his eyes. He'll ask Norton to look in on her again. Judging by the charts, last time she saw the baby was seven days ago.

The doctor leans back in his chair. He'll phone the library, give them some names, get them to do a literature search. He massages his neck and glances at his watch. His son is already in bed. He imagines lifting the telephone receiver to call his wife.

Maggie

Friday night. We lie in each other's arms. We have done the dishes, not talked about the baby. Her presence a terrible, beauteous light that hurts the eyes, that never dissipates, that burns. Skipper leaps onto the bed and knocks against us, breathing out his halitosis. I flip off the bed and put him out. He rains us with indignant whines. While Brodie marked his test papers, back to me at our small dining room table, I tried to read, then tossed the book aside, started baking, then abandoned the chocolate cheesecake brownies, began to clean, an awful restlessness gripping me, until once when I passed Brodie, vacuum and dust cloth in tow, he grabbed my hand, said, Maggie, which led us here. My soft and clingy nightgown, the colour of autumn leaves. Brodie is naked, aroused in sorrow. Maggie. He pulls my nightgown off, reaches, his tongue sliding my skin. He runs his fingers from my hipbone down in against my cradled warmth. I hold on to Brodie's buttocks, slip my hands into their centre. He shakes, a stifled cry. His fingers find my neck, the indent of my backbone, pursue their travelling, roam my small curve of belly, and take flight against me, butterfly-wing light.

Maggie. The most Brodie can say, and then my body arching, arching, he slides down down down down against me, disappears his tongue, invites my cries against his skin. The light is all around.

$p_i \dot{q}_i - L$ where

$\dfrac{\partial H}{\partial p_i}$, $\dot{p}_i = -\dfrac{\partial H}{\partial q_i}$

The Poisson bracket of two variables

$[u, v] = \sum_k \left[\dfrac{\partial u}{\partial q_k} \dfrac{\partial v}{\partial p_k} - \dfrac{\partial u}{\partial p_k} \dfrac{\partial v}{\partial q_k} \right]$ — *two*

Then $\dfrac{du}{dt} = [u, H] + \dfrac{\partial u}{\partial t}$

Inordinate Light

then $\dfrac{du}{dt} = [u, H] + \dfrac{\partial u}{\partial t}$

$\nabla \times \vec{E} + \dfrac{1}{c}\dfrac{\partial \vec{B}}{\partial t} = 0$

$\nabla \cdot \vec{D} = 4\pi\rho$ $\nabla \times \vec{H} - \dfrac{1}{c}\dfrac{\partial \vec{D}}{\partial t} = \dfrac{4\pi}{c}\vec{J}$

here $\vec{E}$ = electric field, $\vec{B}$ = magnetic field
$\vec{D} = \vec{E} + 4\pi\vec{P}$, $\vec{H} = \vec{B} - 4\pi\vec{M}$

$\nabla \cdot \vec{B} = 0$ $\nabla \times \vec{E} + \dfrac{1}{c}\dfrac{\partial \vec{B}}{\partial t} = 0$

$\nabla \cdot \vec{E} = 0$ $\nabla \times \vec{B} - \dfrac{1}{c}\dfrac{\partial \vec{E}}{\partial t} = 0$

$\nabla^2 \vec{E} - \dfrac{1}{c^2}\dfrac{\partial^2 \vec{E}}{\partial t^2}$

$\vec{E} = \vec{E}_0 e$

Maggie

Stilled birds shake themselves into currents of song as I move through the dim house early this morning, past the spiral of Brodie's breathing, to sit shivering in the bare outline of my living room. What do I know of grief? Seeing through a glass darkly. *When I was a child, I spake as a child, I thought as a child, I reasoned as a child. When I became an adult, I put away childish things—*

Once, I believed grief was pure and simple: sadness. No one warned me of aching muscles, dull depression, headaches, bitter isolation. I look out the window to the empty street and think of Char. First year of university. Four in the morning, a high-pitched keening, a banging on my dorm door. Char, crazy, laughing Char, my new Toronto friend who kissed me on the mouth when I sat on the toilet at a house party the night before. Char stumbling into my room, clambering into my bed, dragging lament behind her, one long-held note, an alphabet of sound. Din filled my room, my groggy head, my need to shush her, Char's cold hands shattering my sleep, grabbing my skin, her cries sailing, alive. I struggled to sit up. Her treble wrenched off like a tap.

Maggie! Voice urgent, low now. Tell me what to do! What do? The tortured eyes. Maggie, help — I don't know how to grieve.

I learned the news over breakfast gossip in the cafeteria, Char sleeping like one drugged within my crumpled sheets. Char's estranged dad, murdered in Mexico. Died of a stab wound to the heart.

I long for such a spill of blood. A proof of suffering. A measurement of grief.

I look at my watch, Brodie will be starting second period. Three hours gone.

These days, in the hospital, the supermarket, the bank, a tide of unmitigated misery holds me hostage, wells tight against my rib cage, fills my chest like thick black tar. Light sears my eyeballs. I have surrendered my baby to people who do not love her, people whose job it is to hurt her.

Your grief is going to kill you, the Dutch nurse said two days ago as she adjusted the drip on Kalila's Prosobee. They'd stuck a baby bottle nipple in her mouth, taped on the back to hold out air. She was sucking furiously. She looked so cute. The scene so somehow normal.

Your body won't stand this. The nurse grabbed an Opsite bandage and wrapped the baby's arm. You're here too much, she said. As if grief were a job, and I could punch out at five o'clock or, better yet, put in my notice. This is the nurse who jokes that Kalila must not listen to her. You don't want to grow up speaking like me, now, she will say in her guttural English, covering the baby's ears and laughing. She reconnected the heart monitor and said, You know, it's only in North America people *expect* children to live.

And now I've broken out in three cold sores. Won't be allowed on the neonatal floor for seven days. I'm dangerous. Life floats on. Do the shopping, wash the car, take Skipper to the vet, the dog's hair is falling out, they don't know why, buy Brodie a Cross pen, my mother's motto, *you can always take one more step*, make supper, old hymns rattling round my head. *What a fellowship, what a joy divine, leaning on the everlasting arms*... What can I lean on? Evidently nothing.

Brodie goes to school, drives to the hospital. I'm home alone days, nights, walking a darkened house, can't bear the lights on. I pounce on Brodie the moment he returns. Silent Brodie turned reporter. Tonight he bathed the baby, the site around her gastrostomy tube is red and hardened, her intravenous is fastened in her left hand, she slept, she awoke, her hair grew, there was a spina bifida scare, but it's been ruled out, she's on thirty-two per cent oxygen, twenty-eight per cent oxygen, tomorrow she's having a barium swallow, Brodie doesn't know why.

This banished week I step into the surprise of early winter, run Skipper on the hill. Skipper's hair loss is the beginnings of eczema, from acute anxiety, the vet phones to say. His tone is disapproving, as if I torture the dog. I see Vs of wild geese escaping south, a sailing sparrow's shimmer as he darts past winter's grip. When I come back inside, I do the wash, water my dried-up plants, actually sweep, vacuum the green-flecked carpet, stand at the window and watch the neighbour's little girl make snow angels, a crazy chain of songs squeezing a vise around my head. *Only Je-sus can mend a broken heart ...Close up the casement, Shut out that stealing moon...You promised to buy me a bonny blue ribbon...* My need for Brodie so great that when he walks in the door each night, ripe with hospital experience, I want to hit him, drive him to distraction with my questions. Today the news is good. The baby's coronary arteries are normal in position and distribution. They've done a test. Her abdominal contents show unremarkable. I follow him as he hangs up his sports jacket, gets a glass of water, riffles through the mail.

But did they say more about her enlarged liver, Brodie? Does she still have the rash on her buttocks? Is her temperature up? What about her gastrostomy? Well, is it leaking? What yellow drainage? Her alarm went off three times? What for, Brodie? What do you mean, you didn't check?

I berate him for holding Kalila too much, for not holding her enough. For what he didn't say, did say to the doctors, until, worn out from all their movement, my cold sores crack and weep. Brodie, ghost-faced, rises and goes to bed, his lab reports unmarked. I stand at the window, my womb an ice wind blowing.

When I sleep, I dream dogs. A dog fettered to a schoolyard fence. A dog stuffed in a burning fireplace. A dog with his chest cavity ripped open. A dog falling out of a speeding van door. A dog with diarrhea on Brodie's mother's rug. I wake, dreaming of Houdini, of magical escape. Toss until dawn burns crimson the morning sky. Magicians, the doctors. They hold the big trick in the bag.

I look around my house this banished week, at my novels, my vases, my mismatched towels, my photo albums, my knick-knacks from our trip to Venice, my scented candles, my paintings on the wall, with the frightening clarity of someone who could just walk out. Abandon. Leave it all behind.

For seven days Brodie dutifully gathers information, accumulates detail, speaks. We were just wondering, um, if there is any news?

The doctor stands in light, skin smooth and fine, eyes bland, waiting for this new dad to finish so he can pick up sushi, make a phone call, carry out another procedure, attend the Philharmonic, work on his stamp collection, watch his daughter's soccer game, practise his Italian, sleep.

There are moments, rare, but moments when we forget. Me, on waking, Brodie, shovelling the walk. The phone rings. A friend, a minister, a second cousin on my mother's side.

Hello?

Maggie.

The pregnant pause.

How *are* you?

And I turn and look out on bleak November streets, the threads of my dress sucking through my skin to infiltrate my cells, my tissues, bloodstream.

I learn not to look ahead. There's nothing out there. My body belongs nowhere, not at the hospital with the baby, not at home without the baby. My body has betrayed me, thinned. I want its outline to say, I have a baby, and for that to be an ordinary sentence. Instead, I look out on a snow-fused world from this body that bears no inscriptions of punishment, no sagging stomach, no rounded milk breasts, no angry stretch marks. My father, shortly before he died, the cancer diminishing his body until he took up no space at all, opened his eyes one evening and said so quietly, I'd like to live. He insisted on clearing the rolling table on which he kept his books and papers for the hair-netted worker each time she brought his meal, as if affording her a kind of pity for witnessing his demise. He lost his life, people say. Misplaced it.

To lose. *Webster's New Ninth Collegiate*. To loosen and dissolve. Almost six weeks have passed and the detail is all wrong. The baby's lungs won't breathe without pumped-in oxygen, her heart won't course blood into the proper arteries, her muscles won't summon the strength to lift her head; her skin is blue. My body perfects itself while the baby's scars and bruises write themselves on skin.

My body isn't acting like a mother's body. Mothers don't cry, they take care of the crying. Mothers hold babies in their arms. I shouldn't have had that second piece of chocolate cheesecake in my third month, I shouldn't have jogged so much, I should have jogged more, I should have read more books on birthing. The hooks behind the kitchen door fill me with empty rage. I'm tied to people I wouldn't look at twice. Receptionists. Lab technicians. Doctors. Nurses. An early winter.

Snow crying to the ground.

Maggie

It's not a question of lowering our expectations. On the radio, driving to the hospital, a man says, Humans have to have a culture in order to survive. You don't have to be cruel to be a torturer, he says, you just have to be obedient. Seven p.m. A long, bleak night. The baby's intravenous went interstitial again. She's aspirated again. They've had to turn up her oxygen. Babies go blind from too much oxygen. Mottled green bruises lace her scalp and hands. Six needles plucked from her scalp in a twenty-minute period. Let's try this again! the hearty nurse says.

The man on the radio said, We have to *believe* the things that matter to us are going to survive.

I remember studying the word *believe* for a spelling test, mixing the *e* and the *i*.

There's a lie in believe, Maggie, my mother said.

Brodie

You tuck your blue-and-green checked shirt — a Brodie shirt, Maggie's sisters call it — into your green flannel pants and say, Okay. Question number ten. What concept does this question deal with?

Uniform motion, a scattering of voices calls.

And uniform motion is?

Motion at a constant speed.

Thank you, Eileen. And speed, as not many of you have learned, judging by the number of you who got this test question wrong, equals distance over time. You scribble the equation on the blackboard. Harold, read the question.

Brodie and Maggie took their dog for a walk at the river. When they parked the car, Brodie got out and started walking. Maggie remained behind to gather up the leash and doggie bags and lock up the car. Skipper, worried that Brodie and Maggie would become separated, ran full tilt back and forth between them on the path. Maggie took three minutes to lock up the car. If Brodie was walking five kilometres per hour, and three minutes later, Maggie began walking seven kilometres per hour, how far would Skipper, bounding at twenty kilometres per hour, have to run before Maggie caught up to Brodie?

Hey, Mr. Solantz, is Maggie your wife?

Mr. Solantz, you have a dog?

What kind is she?

Mr. Solantz is married? I never knew he was married. You're married, Mr. Solantz?

She is, I do, I am, and she's a he. And details of Skipper's daily habits, or mine, are not going to help you pass your physics departmental.

Skipper! Is he a mongrel?

You sigh. Last question, Anita. Promise? He's a springer spaniel.

Awwwwww, echoes around the classroom. They're so cute.

And smart, Anita says. I read that —

Anita, Skipper's smart. He could probably pass this physics exam. The question is, Could you? Now help me work out this question. Where do we begin?

Well, says a gum-snapping Anita, *I'd* begin with the character of Brodie. Why the hell would he leave Maggie to lock up the car like that? He just walked off on her? Why would Maggie even want to catch up with the jerk? Anita slumps back in her chair. I tell you what I'd do. I'd drive right off and leave him!

You pull at your hair in mock anguish. This is about speed that *doesn't* change, okay? They all have to move at their own rate so you can work out the problem. Forget the character of Brodie. I'll work on his manners for the next exam. Come up here, Anita, and solve the problem.

I was only trying to *express myself*, Anita says, eyes feigning innocence, blue and sparkling.

You want to take these happy people in your arms.

Maggie

Suzette and Francine, dripping costume jewellery, wiggle up beside me at my kitchen table in their dress-up clothes. Francine hiccups and inhales two snuffly breaths. I pour my nieces pretend green tea. Skipper rams his head under my elbow. Kool-Aid splashes.

Remember this tea set, Maggie, when we were little? Marigold wipes up the spills. Skipper, shoo! Auntie Maggie and I drank from this set when we were little girls. We had a wooden-egg-crate table in that red peeling granary.

What's an egg crate? asks Suzette, licking her green-stained mouth.

What's a granary? mutters Francine.

Skipper helps himself to the Nanaimo bar hanging squished between Francine's dangling fingers.

City kids! Marigold scoffs. A granary is a square little building where a farmer stores his wheat. That's what bread is made from, only this granary was empty — except for chaff. Grandpa gave it to us for a playhouse.

And Grandma sewed us curtains out of flour sacks —

Out of *what*?

Really, I give up! Marigold laughs. She tweaks Francine's brunette braids. It's what flour came in, great woven bags; you use flour to make bread.

You said wheat makes bread, Francine says sulkily.

I'm sorry your rabbit died, Francine, Marigold says cheerily, but let's not be rude. Grandma made us a flour-sack-tableclo — I miss To-oo-ops, Francine quavers, knocking over her lime Kool-Aid. Suzette lets out a sympathetic howl.

Honey, rabbits die when they get old. Marigold helps herself to a scone. To mitigate their grief, the girls go for thirds of my quick-thawed Nanaimo bars.

He didn't suffer. Marigold curls Francine's damp bangs around a finger. Come, sit here, sweets, to Suzette.

Suzette curls against her mom and takes a bite. We found Tops this morning with his teeth like this — head against Marigold's breast, Suzette bucks her teeth, chocolate oozing. He was flopped in his cage, ears stuck straight out. Suzette falls sideways against her chair and holds the pose. Plum dead and gone. She takes a gulp of Kool-Aid. Coughs.

Francine swallows a cranky belch. Auntie Maggie, is your baby going to die? She isn't even *old!*

Time pushing out like kilometres. Cousin Danny's grade ten photograph perched on his coffin at the front of the country church, his smile a light shining on the congregation as they looked back and wept. Uncle Ty leaning heavy on

Auntie Prue's arm, his countenance wild and in motion. Farmers, wives in Sunday best, pouring like a river into our country church.

We sang, the Watson girls. Marigold and I, soprano, Rose, high tenor, Iris carried the alto. June galloping the piano.

> *Under His wings, I am safely abiding,*
> *Though the night deepens and tempests are wild…*

Danny had drawn a picture in art class, a flock of wild geese rising in blue sky. The teacher drove it out to Uncle Ty's farm and handed it over, one last gift from Danny, *the least that she could do.* The minister taped the drawing behind the pulpit. Later, Auntie Prue and Uncle Ty had it transcribed onto Danny's gravestone. Engraved above the birds's flight, *Safe under the shelter of thy wings.*

I believed it.

Marigold, gently gathering up their things and ushering out the girls. Come, honey, come on, girls, no, Auntie Maggie needs to be alone.

✦

My stomach skidded with strange excitement at the sadness that engulfed the congregation, like a shiver without release, as we sang, the Watson girls, to a church chock full, intent, grief-stricken faces, the overflow crowd pressed together in the foyer, down the stairs, and out the door into the churchyard.

Under His wings, under His wings
Who from His lo-ove can sever...

I breathe in the pulse of Danny's funeral, the gusty hymns, the storm of sobbing, heat rising like a fever. Marigold and I played frozen tag with Danny's sisters between the funeral and lunch. Warm comfort of mini cabbage rolls, buns and sausage, cherry squares, and bundt cake, which migrated us all together in Auntie Prue's cheery sunlit kitchen. The church women bustling, counting teacups, clucking, sighing, arranging cheese and salami platters while Marigold and I and Danny's little sisters dashed through the kitchen, stealing lemon meringue tarts on the run. Over the years we climbed on Danny's gravestone, played leapfrog over it, drank Freshie and ate homemade cookies on it during vacation Bible school. It never made me sad. This gathering before the dead seemed natural, sustaining, like the expectation of pale shoots in the potato bin's dim corner of the cellar. We ran barefoot through the tended grass, stopped to read the gravestones: Orkney Island Schallhorn, 1923–1925, *Little Lamb of God*; Ida E. Alberta, 1935–1967, *Loving wife and mother*; Cyrus Persida, *In Him We Have Our Rest.* Joseph Callan, June 1914–September 1914, *Tread Gently. A Dream Lies Buried Here.* And I imagined extraordinary lives in extraordinary worlds. Death a mere curiosity, an intriguing step beyond.

While Uncle Ty moved through that July and August in

a kind of stunned persistence, his love for his remaining children grew desperate, each earache a potential deafness, each sore throat, meningitis. Stuffed full of vitamins, antibiotics, antihistamines, the cousins played.

I cheerfully killed off my dolls one by one: drowned Hazel in the water trough, climbed the windmill and flung Rosella, suffocated Betty in the woodbox. Marigold and I held funerals on the cellar stairs, which made great church pews. Iris and Rose joined in when they had exhausted themselves in tag, anti-i-over, and scrub. The coveted roles gravitated between the grieving mother and the chorister. It was heart-rending to quaver,

> *Our path strewn with stones, We cry in despair*
> *Lord do not forsake us, Oh Lord, are you there?*

So thrilling that by the chorus end, the Watson girls were sobbing,

> *Kneel at the cross and feel His arms embrace us*
> *Kneel at the cross and our burdens He'll bear…*

The lovely melodrama. Mom would appear at the head of the cellar stairs, Och, what do I do with the lot of you? Assuaging the headaches and achy throats that accompanied such blasts of grief. She'd make us honey ginger tea and vinegar punch. I've never seen the like, she'd scold. I've never seen the like. And my sisters and I, delighted we'd played our parts so well, would dash off for a game of alley alley home free on the front lawn, leaving little stashes of soggy tissues on the cellar steps for Mom to scoop up when she went to the basement to fetch a jar of peaches or to check the cheese. That fall, I raised every doll from the dead.

Maggie

The baby is seven weeks old when we attend a party for Brodie's high-school staff. Maggie, Brodie begging. Please? We need to get out.

A woman at the party pops a strawberry in her mouth, says, Well, I would have sworn someone said you'd had a baby.

I did, I say. I do.

You've had a baby? The woman stares at my flat stomach. God! Milt. Come look at Brodie Solantz's skinny wife. She's had a baby!

I say, I have the afterbirth to prove it.

The woman loses her next sentence, has more wine.

I stand alone on the edge of the dance floor, reciting book titles in my head: *My Heart is Broken, Setting Free the Bears, Politics and the English Language, The Angel in the House, October Light, To All Appearances a Lady.* I think of fairy tales, where good mothers die before the story starts.

Unmother. I spilled my blood onto the birthing table,

then someone whisked away the baby: nineteen hours and I haven't seen her. The first fourteen strapped to my bed by two intravenous needles, one in each hand, to stop the bleeding. There are babies everywhere. I peer beneath small blankets on the rolling cribs that cruise the hall. People steal babies from hospitals. Mothers stare. I've taken two sitz baths today. I feel a fraud when I occupy the sitz bath, when I enter like a thief its enclosed heat. There are the mothers, and then there's me. Nothing dislodges their identity. What right have I to complain of bleeding stitches in my episiotomy? Mothers have episiotomies. I'm an aberrant, like being two sexes at once. A mother, not a mother. A nurse buzzes my bedside. The intercom crackles. Your kid's crying in the nursery, a frazzled voice comes through. A small intake of breath. Sorry. Wrong number. Could you tell your roommate her kid's crying in the nursery?

Here comes Brodie across the gymnasium floor, heading from the bar carrying an offering of translucent garnet punch. My breasts sting. Guest. Host. Parasite. The doctors the host, me the parasite. Kalila, their unwanted guest. I can hear her hoarse and whispered cries over the slap of the woman's slippers from the adjoining bed as she pushes past her husband.

Well, why don't I just do every goddamn thing myself? The woman flings over her shoulder and sweeps out the door.

The husband shoots me a look of such resentment. Maggie Watson, hospital soap star. My body tightens around a cramp. It's too late for love at first sight. How sick is my baby?

A nurse checks the drip. Come on now, Mrs. Solantz. You'll be back to normal in no time.

Normal. My pleasure body has brought everything to this.

Roses. Brodie brings me roses. Their sad and choking smell hangs in hospital air. Before the child was born, I said, And you must buy me roses. A dozen of them bloom with mad abandon in this sterile room.

Brodie bumps my elbow, hands me the punch. Around us dancers bebop, forty-year-old balding men, trying for cool. An open window. The stuffy air creeps damp under my skin. Outside on the street a truck gears down, rolls by, and we're wrapped in sudden diesel fumes, eyes smarting in dim and raw fluorescent light. Brodie takes me in his arms. We step into the music. We have ignored the dessert table, with its chocolate-dipped strawberries, its petit fours, its custard tarts.

Tonight we dance the two-step, side by side, alone.

Brodie

Your mother is not ten minutes in the house before she tells you the child did not sprout from your genes. Not her Irish genes, anyway.

She's scrubbing out the sink that you scrubbed out this morning. Her coat flung over a chair. Your parents stay for days. Our genes are strong, your mother says.

You look at your face in the hallway mirror. I thought Aunt Betts had a baby born without a chest.

I don't know how you deal with this disorganization, your mother says. Will somebody put out the damn dog? He keeps tramping on my feet. His breath is terrible! Where do you keep the teapots? That wasn't Aunt Betts. That was on your father's side.

Right, Joyce, your father says. Blame the Solantzes.

On the counter, Maggie says. We keep them on the counter.

You're not putting green pepper in the chicken? Green pepper gives your father gas.

You say, Real gas or ideal gas? and when no one gets your physics joke — I'll get the car out.

✢

At the hospital, Joyce is put out by the smallness of the scrub room. There is a jar of flowers, daffodils and daisies, sitting on the coffee table in green water, as if someone got mixed up and thought it might be spring. Your father needs help getting the string tied on his gown. He makes jokes about being in a nightie, about the pretty nurses.

We have to wash up, Dad.

Larry's hand rests on the door handle. What are we? Contaminated?

You herd them in and along the crowded aisles.

The child's awake today.

Say hello to your grandma and grandpa, you say gently to the baby.

Joyce and Larry stare. The baby closes her eyes.

They're so wrinkled! Joyce, eyes flitting everywhere at bodies covered in tape, tubes sticking out of throats. At least yours looks *kind* of normal.

They're the size of goddamn roasting chickens, your father breathes.

Hi, baby! Joyce shouts through the armholes, jolting the baby, startling nearby nurses. She eyes the tubes and needles. Hi, baby! It's Granny! How the hell do you get her out?

You open the isolette lid, arrange the tubes that bind her,

hold your child out to your father, whose feet don't want to move.

Larry! Joyce says, and Larry's feet unglue.

You snap pictures of Larry, arms filled with the tiny lump of blanket. The oxygen tube slips from the baby's nose onto the floor. Her skin is chafed and raw around her gastrostomy site.

Joyce rescues Larry. You snap more pictures, hand the camera to Maggie, who shoots photos of you and your father flanking your mother, baby clamped against her. Say pickle! Joyce says into the baby's face. A family moment.

Okay, here, Joyce thrusts at you the swath of blanket. Larry needs to keep on schedule for his diabetes. Let's go home and eat. Goodbye! Goodbye! she sings, flapping her arms inside the isolette. The baby breathes a rattly sigh.

On your way out, a floor washer causes you to make a detour past the normal nursery. Joyce peers through the window. Look at that Pakistani baby crying.

Mom, you say wearily, babies don't cry because of the colour of their skin.

You step through the sliding doors and into endless winter.

Maggie

Iris phones from Ottawa. Her concern crackles down the wire. She and Ed drove to the Gatineau Hills this weekend. The colours were spectacular. This morning she's been making playdough for her preschool class. Emily's caught the flu. Yesterday Iris took her to the doctor. She's home from school today. They are forecasting high winds. Maggie, what can I do to help?

The radio is playing, *I want you to tell me why you walked out on me.*

The morning sun a cheerful flush against Nose Hill, the barren trees.

I'm so lonesome every da-ay...

Are things any better? Is there any news?

The doctor says she has right ventricle hypertrophy.

What?

Her heart is enlarged, Iris. And she has pulmonary hypertension.

Maggie, you have to speak my language.

Her lungs aren't working right, okay? Her blood pressure is way too high. She has too much fluid. They don't know why. And now they've found her left kidney's not developed.

Skipper shoves against me.

> *Walk right back to me this minute,*
> *Bring your love to me, don't send it...*

I am crying, and Iris begins to cry, and we chalk up tears at thirty-seven cents a minute while outside people scrape their sidewalks and enter taxis, light cigarettes, someone holds up a bank on Centre Street, a woman murders a man in an apartment complex, and children dash along the river hand in hand.

Maggie

I cart language around this foreign landscape.

What's that tube doing up my baby's nose? Why is a neurosurgeon checking her out? She's not #524010. She's not Baby Solantz. This baby has a name. Kalila. Why didn't someone say she needed a hearing test? Why can't you find the vein?

The nurses chat among themselves. The mother-in-law of the redhead dislikes her, always has. The big one with the neck scar touts the merits of microfibre cloths over paper towels. The freckled one orders shoes online. You can do returns if they don't fit.

Dr. Vanioc strides down the hall. I feel the urge to break and enter, take an axe, smash barriers down. Can we talk?

Dr. Vanioc skids to a stop.

What's apnea?

When a baby forgets to breathe, Mrs. Solantz.

Watson. What are bradys?

Severe apnea can lead to bradycardia, a dangerous slowing of the heart rate. He glances at his watch.

You mean it might stop?

He looks at me.

What's interstitial?

Fluid sometimes seeps into the tissue. We're careful as we can be.

You mean the skin?

I mean the tissue.

Will that kill her?

Mrs. Solantz, it just swells up the tissue.

She's doing *relatively* well, *but*... She's *some* better today, *although*... Today's results are *somewhat* optimistic, *yet*...

I cling to intensifiers and conjunctions. What's wrong with her? It's been nine weeks. Can you just give it a name? Didn't have my hand up. Spoke out of turn. I'll be sent back to the social worker's office. Nope. Not going there. Babies airlifted here from Brooks, Nanton, the Porcupine Hills, from Field, B.C., dropped down in Calgary sunlight from place names that conjure pure spring water, fresh earth, mountain streams, healthy outdoors. Babies spin down corridors past oatmeal-coloured walls, a collection of nurses bagging on the run, heralding another birth, a forlorn father staring from the birthing room door.

Don't expect a forecast. The weather here is unpredictable.

I turn my back, walk out the hospital doors, drive to a

bookstore, buy myself *Cartright's Medical Home Dictionary*. A thousand pages. Four pounds. To hell with them, I'll learn the language myself.

I stop at the bank, mail electricity and gas bills, fill the car, wind tearing at my clothes, pay library fines, pick up a windshield scraper, renew *Maclean's*, buy Brodie garlic pills. The airwaves resonate with heartache: a gang of teenaged boys' tough bravado, a woman in an electric wheelchair hailing a cab, a couple standing in Mark's Work Warehouse, fighting about jeans. I head for the grocery store. My gaping heart. Like Jesus's, it has no protective cover.

Brodie

You help Maggie chop carrots for the stew. Her arms,
their sculpted outline, their scattering of freckles. Her neck
muscles clenching. You're lonely for her, even though she's
here. She reaches for an onion and soon begins to cry, bent
over, fists stuffed in eyesockets, laughing, It hurts. It hurts.
You want to buy her a silver necklace you cannot afford, a
pair of ruby earrings, something to draw her breath in, clasp
her hands together. Something to make her forget, if only
for a little while. Her arms make angular shadow puppets
against the wall. Winter dusk brings sadness, a despondency
you have to fight. Pushes you to silence. Maggie gets pissed
off that you don't chat, but these days you're holding up the
world.

She hands you celery. You begin to chop. You are an out-
sider; you've always been. Your parents use words to inflict
damage, like the side of an axe to drive a point home. Words
frighten you. A phrase falls like Newton's apple, drops and

explodes before you get it out; words shift into shapes, intents you never meant. In the classroom this doesn't happen, only here, where words are too important. Galileo left words altogether. In the late 1500s he disappeared into the Camaldolese monastery; attracted by the quiet, studious life, he joined the order.

You start in on the Chinese cabbage. People in ancient times believed the earth stood still, and the sky moved around it. That's how they explained the changing position of the stars, movement from night to day. Strange, the earth's steadfast rotation. Exactly three hundred and sixty-five days, six hours, nine minutes, and ten seconds. One revolution around the sun. You'll put that on the grade ten science exam. You pick up a zucchini. A trivia bonus question.

Maggie climbs a chair to reach a serving bowl. You want to say, I'll tell you anything, but Maggie doesn't ask. Beside you, your Cross pen, three red marking pens, your calculator, a stone you picked up by the river, your labs, a book called simply *Physics*, as if that says it all. Maggie moves to the light switch and, without asking, gathers up your pens and papers, sets a place for two.

She's using few words these days. You miss her chatter, her foolish endless lists of who she lunched with, a joke one of the old men in the Home told her — why is six afraid of seven? Because seven eight nine — how some of the old ladies are forever chasing Fred Regier. Those times seem relics of an ancient world that you strain to remember.

Throughout dinner neither of you says a thing.
Your silence, and the rhythm of the lifting of your spoons.

three

Refraction

Maggie

Foothills Neonatal ICU becomes a separate country. With its own time zones, population, weather. Well-behaved mothers are allowed inside its borders only after passport inspection, the ritual washing, the donning of the gown.

The hospital gown: that barrier, that disguise. A yellow gown that forces mothers to look like invalids, not real mothers at all. What does a mother bring to neonatal? Nothing. I flip open the Mother File in the filing cabinet of my head, watch my own, bent weeding in the garden, moving under loads of wash, sprinkling clothes, making soap, cutting noodles, gutting chickens, canning fruit, alive with the energy of chores. My mother fed her children from the soil. I pushed my child, soiled, into the world. She slid out in her own feces, meconium-stained. A sign of distress, the doctors said. Kalila made some pick of a mom. I look around the huge warehouse of a room, designed for optimal efficiency. Isolettes jut from the walls. Panels of wall plugs. Blinking, beeping monitors. Hell of a nursery I've created for my daughter. The nurses told me yesterday they'll take no more breast milk. Kalila cannot swallow. Just give up the breast pump. There's no work I'm allowed to do. Not even fold clothes. Kalila has none. My work experience in a seniors' residence doesn't translate to this place. The neonatal nursery doesn't want a program coordinator to set up crafts, exercise classes, book displays for two-pound babies the size of a hunk of cheese. It doesn't want parents who stick their noses in the doctors' business. I pass through the quarantine room, sidestep a large basket of soiled gowns. The mothers' job here in Foothills Neonatal is to stand around in yellow gowns like a hospital choir. If nothing else we are clean. What would the nurses do if we broke into song?

> *I'm so lonesome for you, baby*
> *I'm so lonesome all the time...*

The smell of camphor salve, digoxin, formaldehyde, wet diapers, fear.

> *You're my dream come true*
> *I cry through empty nights withou-ou-out you...*

I fight my way this morning among the babies and equipment to find Kalila, awake and waiting, left hand ballooned and purple.

What happened?

Her intravenous went interstitial.

Interstitial: occupying the place between.

Nothing serious, nurses cry over their shoulders, bagging, resuscitating, administering physiotherapy and drugs.

I look through glass at my child. #524010 with the swollen hand.

You'll have to leave now, Mrs. Solantz.

A bird, long-beaked and blue, soars by the high window and wheels away. I have a sudden image of my flock of sisters: Marigold, Iris, Rose, June, crowding, chattering, interrupting, talking while they chew, their language tumbling, intimate, inclusive. Someone has opened the door to the hall, but still, the bleach-tinged air. The closed-up smell of things unsaid. The doctors here navigate the crowded aisles in a choreographed line dance to avoid questions. They bend over procedures, backs turned, faces guarded. Where dancers open their bodies, the doctors shut theirs off, their movements exclusive, circling inward. It is always high noon here, always glaring light. When forced, the doctors speak in codes of graphs and charts, prescriptions, lab results.

Your daughter has multiple problems, Mrs. Solantz, many undiagnosed at present.

There is a swallowing disturbance (a disturbance? like a fucking cold front?) and abnormal electroencephalogram.

How do you spell that?

A startled doctor spells.

At this time, your daughter appears to have pulmonary dysplasia and so is in danger of potential sepsis.

I scribble.

She has intermittent cyanosis. We hear rhonchi and rales in her chest.

Her presence reminds them they are failing.

I want to see her.

I'm sorry, Mrs. Solantz, you'll have to leave this morning.

I long for emotion from them; what they want from me is none. This is a research hospital. My baby is useful.

Ma'am, the doctors have their rounds to do. All case information is confidential.

I imagine myself one day fading toward the exit, melting out the sliding doors, vanishing to nothing. I feel it coming, my body, dissolving into light.

Pretend you're not here, I tell myself. *They* do.

Before I can grab my purse, say my goodbyes, the march of the white coats begins. Bona fide doctors in long coats lead trailing residents in short. They swing from isolette to isolette, their cryptic voices. They stare at the babies, comment, prod, confer. Move to Baby Hargreaves, the size of two blocks of butter, sparrow legs dry, the tendons showing, to Baby Mueller, a fourteen-pound elephant, brain damaged as he ploughed his way through his diabetic mother's birth canal, to Baby Leung, born without an anus.

I take a last look at their white backs and file out with the other parents, passive as babies. Two go home, one walks the halls, I look up words in my dictionary in an empty waiting room.

Electroencephalogram, EEG: records the minute electrical impulses produced by the activity of the brain. Indicates the alertness of the subject.

Pulmonary dysplasia: any abnormality of growth. She has abnormal lungs, then. No one's said.

I wait. That's all. I wait. Day after week. Emigrant turned immigrant, yoked to this hospital.

> *Whither thou goest I will go*
> *Wherever thou lodgest I will lodge*
> *Thy people will be my people, my love.*

Yoked to this dreaded family of sick babies, prim receptionists, smoking relatives, green-suited floor polishers, anxious nurses, taciturn doctors.

A mother enters the waiting room, a runny-nosed three-year-old whining at her leg. Hands smoothing her daughter's fruit-embroidered dress, she tells me the hospital is threatening foster care if she doesn't visit her baby more often.

They're telling me my constant presence is getting in the way.

Sepsis: infection of a wound or body tissues with bacteria.

Cyanosis: a bluish colouration of the skin and mucus membrane. A sign of heart disorder, lung damage, fluid in the lungs.

I want to strike at the thick smoke of their secrets.

> *If I didn't care*
> *More than words can say…*

The mother stands, watching me write. The child wants to colour in my dictionary.

My dictionary won't transform itself into pretty pictures.

What's wrong with *your* baby then? the child says.

What a question! Let's fill in the blanks. Give us an E, Vanna. Are there any Es?

Does she look funny? Does your baby smell? *Ours* does. Today…

The mother takes the child's arm, turns her away, covers the child's eyes.

> *Peek a boo,* singsongs the mother,
> *I see you,*
> *No, I don't!*
> *Yes, I do!!*

What kind of psycho made up a disappearing baby game?

Rhonchi: a rattling.

Rales: an abnormal sound heard on auscultation of the chest.

Auscultation: listening to the heart, lungs, organs with a stethoscope.

Once, I was safe. Once, I owned myself. Now, not even my grief is mine. The hospital owns it. I can rent, make withdrawals, like books on a library card. Time's up. Hand it over. Bear it. Buck up. Grow up. Quit snivelling. A headache at the centre of the storm. I want to strike at them. Instead I put my arms into my coat and carry my four-pound dictionary out into the ordinary world, into the harsh cold swell of winter. Ache in the gut. Pretend you chose this. Pretend you deserve this. It makes the explosions in the lungs easier to bear.

Brodie

You walk the railroad tracks while Skipper bounds into the bushes, scares out birds, and splashes into the river, barking. You throw a stick. Sunlight travels the water. Skipper, tail spinning propellerlike, retrieves, and, coughing, gagging, throat-clearing, aims his bedraggled self toward shore, but the current carries him downstream and, thrashing sideways, he disappears. After some time you hear him crashing through the bush and here he is, stick clamped between his teeth. He drops it at your feet, shakes himself all over your shoes. When you make to throw the stick again, Skipper snatches it up, and there ensues a tug-of-war, Skipper growling, tail wagging, till you wrest it free and fling the stick again.

The path here in Edworthy Park is lined by caragana bushes, dying with autumn. The intensity of a light wave follows the inverse square law. It radiates out from the source, the intensity decreasing as it travels through space. Science is how you separate truth from ideology, from foolish, unproven beliefs. Physics governs the world you used to know. That world has shifted, tilted off its orbit. You have stumbled into a universe of uncertainty. What porthole will see you through? The wind sings in the trees. You read somewhere that Australian aboriginals believe the world was sung into existence, that their belief system holds song lines, pathways that connect the landscape to a story each life tells. You picture yourself standing in these caragana bushes, lifting your voice to the stars. You smile ruefully. You can't carry a tune. The article said each geographic contour emits its own unique song. You stand still, listen to the grasses. Once, you knew what questions needed asking. Science brought you that. Wind shushes in the trees. The splash of water. Skipper dives for the stick a woman has thrown for her dog. That poster in your study: *Things You Can Learn From A Dog: Allow the experience of fresh air and wind on your face to be pure ecstasy. Take naps and stretch before rising. If you want what's buried, dig until you find it.* A fish jumps. A bald eagle swoops from nowhere, skims the water, snatches, and glides up a tree branch to feast. The sun climbs the sky. Because we circle the sun, it shows us all its faces. Skipper crashes out of tangled bush and grasses. Unlike the moon, which, circling, shows us the same side. Maggie says you hide parts of yourself from her. You don't, no more than you hide them from yourself. Depression twists down your esophagus like a funnel cloud. You turn abruptly, head back, the wind a whistle in your ears. You bend into its force, crunching and slushing the wet and brittle leaves that scatter in your path while the dog tears through them, skidding in wet decay.

At the van, Skipper whines in anticipation while you hunt for your keys, impatient for life's next experience, no matter what it brings. You give his coat an affectionate ruffle and he leaps inside, heads for his mat, paws and paws it, turns four times in a circle, and, satisfied, slumps down. You check your pant legs. Not that dirty. You drive to the hospital, leave Skipper snoring, ride the elevator, scrub your hands, slip into the yellow gown, seat yourself by the baby.

✦

Once upon a time a small glass castle sat high on a windy hill. The castle lodged a little princess, and its walls and ceiling winked and caught the light. The castle and the countryside around stayed lit up night and day, and whenever the little princess wished, she could gaze out her glass walls to what lay on all sides. Dotting the countryside were other tiny glass castles, each with a little prince or princess lodged inside. But like all glass slippers and glass hills in fairy tales, each glass castle was under a spell: each little prince and princess held captive inside the tiny castles unless the Great Sorcerer decided to set them free.

Few escaped to live outside their castle walls. Day after day the little princess languished alone in her glass castle, high on the windy hill. If visitors came, it was to prod or stare or wave or shout Hello outside the castle fortress. Each castle had two small round portholes that opened to the outside, and from time to time a curious visitor would push a hand through, but this happened so rarely that when it did, the little princess recoiled from the touch.

Imagine the princess's loneliness for no human, only food and drink appeared inside her castle walls. She awoke each day to stare wistfully across the landscape...

Kalila's eyes stay closed. *The Little Prince* is sprawled where someone left it, on the shelf under a neighbouring isolette. You pick up the book, press your face against one armhole, flip through its pages:

> *At sunrise, the sand is the colour of honey... What brought me, then, this sense of grief?*
> *...But I, alas, do not know how to see sheep through the walls of boxes.*

Maggie

Spinal tap; lumbar puncture: a procedure in which a hollow needle is inserted in the lower part of the spinal canal to withdraw cerebrospinal fluid. To diagnose and investigate disorders of the brain and the spinal cord.

Infusion: slow introduction of a substance into a vein.

I lug my dictionary and think of Brodie's hands, which are always travelling, caressing a science book's cover, meandering through his hair, tracing an onion's paper skin. 6:05 p.m.. Brodie stays at school to plan his lessons, mark his labs, comes home in darkness, gulps down his supper. Fingers clenching, unclenching on his knee.

Were the kids good, Brodie?

Fine.

Even his jaw works; the core of his emotion resting in a cheekbone. So small a movement. As if a blizzard blew between us and snatched away our words. He starts the car, drives to the hospital, hearts running on empty we sit beside our child, drive back in silence; Brodie goes to bed.

Desire tingles into nerve endings that reach out my hands to walk the inner seam of his pants just above the knee.

Touch me.

I feel so guilty.

His mouth. The brush of finger against that lower lip. I want to slip my hand into his pocket, remove his wallet, play my fingers in that hidden place between materials, search out the cotton twill of his pants.

I awaken on the couch, back stiff, move to the window, a pool of street light, a lone dog trotting down a sidewalk. Skipper emerges, groggy, from his spot under the table, stretch-yawns, regards me gloomily. We stare out at the darkness of Nose Hill.

> *I will lift up mine eyes unto the hills, from whence*
> *cometh my help.*

There's no help coming.

Maggie, you're on your own.

Brodie

The ancient Greeks saw stars and moons and constellations as their gods and heroes. They prayed to them and sought answers to their prayers. They gazed into the night sky and pondered their own place in the cosmos. They tried to understand what we call science.

You can't just study to be a scientist. In order to hypothesize, a scientist must believe. Believe there is an unknown — not what it is, but that it is. How else can he predict? Science equals curiosity. A scientist can't wait for answers. He has to leave the world he knows and go in search of them. A scientist revels in the contradictions.

You stand before your restless grade elevens, pointer on a timeline you have trailed across the blackboard. Frankie's bed head is rising toward the lights in a kind of frenzied glee.

It was in 1900 that Max Planck, the German physicist, formulated an equation that dealt with the emission of light from a hot surface. He couldn't explain *why* his equation worked.

So what was the use? Sukjeevan, twirling a paper clip. Andy gets up to retrieve a sailing pencil, sits down on a tack deposited neatly by Raj. You ignore his small shriek.

I'm starved, Erika mutters.

Well, Planck felt sure that the tiny emitters of light could only have certain values of energy. So, you tip the pointer against the blackboard, he took a leap. He proposed that radiation was made up of small packets, much as matter is made up of atoms. He called each unit of radiation, 'the quantum, or quanta,' which in Latin means?

How much, Ashton says.

Hungry or not, you can rarely stump these kids. Quantum mechanics is what? A theory that governs the very small, those minuscule pieces from which the universe is made. And for those tiny pieces, the rules of our world do not hold. The uncertainty principle reigns in quantum mechanics.

But what about Planck?

What about him? The man proposed something he couldn't see. He took a chance. Chance based on probability. He *proposed* that radiation is made up of these small packets. Were the physicists of his day impressed? No, they were not. Because he couldn't prove it, they believed Planck a kook. But in 1918 that kook won the Nobel Prize. Thanks to Planck's imaginative thinking, quantum physics entered modern thought.

A wad of paper whaps into the garbage can.

A whispered, Right on!

Freddie, just for you, we know you love your sport, fifteen minutes after school today. A coaching session — no, I'm uninterested in excuses, fifteen minutes in which to perfect your hoop shot. I understand your obsession. I'll be here for you. Three-forty. Sharp.

You move your pointer along the timeline trail. It squeaks and sings.

Caleb, are you listening? Five years later, 1905, a young German physicist, Albert Einstein, verified Planck's findings. But Einstein, too, veered off the safe path and in the process made a discovery that changed our view of the world.

Einstein's Theory of Relativity suggested a brand new view of the universe, based on Planck's quantum theory. He proposed that light moved through space in quantum form. He proposed that light had *at the same time* the properties of a particle and a wave. Sometimes it showed one set of properties; sometimes the other.

Yet this was not the most astounding feature of Einstein's discovery. The most astonishing was his rejection of absolute space and absolute time. All we need to do, Einstein said, is pick a frame of reference against which to set the happenings of the universe. Einstein believed time meanders like a river around the stars and galaxies, slowing and speeding.

Now move forward a decade. Trenton, are you with me? Well, try to look it. Remember mid-term's in five days. Do I review for the hell of it? Niels Bohr, a Dane, carried forward the idea of quantum physics. In 1913, he was first to suggest that the energy of *atoms* are quantized as well. It was Bohrs who discovered that electrons simply shift from one orbit to another, without being seen to travel, existing simultaneously in two different orbits. It's called quantum theory because they make a quantum leap. *Quantum Leap*? You guys watch old TV reruns?

You perch on your desk. The superposition of states of quantum mechanics is truly mysterious, grade elevens. Remember the experiment of two holes in the screen? The light can zip through both holes at the same time, instead of having to choose one over the other. Yes, the impossible can occur: a photon, a quantum of light in other words, can be in two or more states, here and there, at the same time.

That doesn't make sense, a voice pipes from the back.

Sure it does. Anita leans forward. It's like my boyfriend — nice guy, son of a bitch —

Anita, you get my gist. Reflect, grade elevens, on how far quantum mechanics has brought us. Humankind has moved from gazing in awe at the unattainable and distant sky, to a particular and detailed study of what light might be, melding the poetry and mystery of the heavens, to the rational logic of scientific inquiry.

Maggie

Mid afternoon light washes the window. Everything ghosts white. I expect the scent of calla lily, trillium, jasmine, snow, picture my mother, standing motionless in a gauze curtain of thought, then turning to finish the dishes at her small sink, feeling their way through grey light into the cupboard. Last night she phoned to say she dreamed she was tattooed in large words and people read her. The dream awash in colour. My dad gone ten years and still Mom's house in town feels strange and new though she's been in it six. Each day her world fades deeper into grey-white twilight. Frost stars the ground. She spends less time with her large-print books, more afternoons listening to old tapes. This morning, she said over the crackling telephone wire, she came across one of us girls singing. She pressed Play, leaned into the window, and my dad appeared. I saw Wilf, bent forward on the chester-field across from the piano, grinning at you girls. His voice lurks in the shadows by the coat hooks, his step on the cellar stairs, she smells his Sen-Sen though she keeps none in the house. Remember, Maggie? She hummed, then sang across the wire:

> When the sun in the morning peeps over the hill,
> And kisses the roses round my windowsill
> Then my heart fills with gladness...

My mother, imagining colour. The brown of a lonesome cowboy song, the soft mauve of a hymn, the wagon-red of "Way Up High in the Cherry Tree." She used to sing that song to us when we couldn't sleep.

> Way up high in the cherry tree
> If you look, you will see
> Mama Robin and babies three...

Song calmed me, after shouting out my childhood nightmares.

Mom had an eye specialist appointment in the city yesterday, she said. The Sawatskys drove her up. The doctor said, Congratulations, Mrs. Watson. You have excellent sight. You're registering 20-25 in both eyes. Quite a feat for someone your age.

Och, why can't I see then? my mother said.

You have macular degeneration, Mom, I reminded her gently. Your retina is full of tiny holes.

Do you know what the doctor told me? my mother said, exasperation in her voice. If you stare sideways long enough, things may grow clear.

Maggie

I want to report a missing child.

I sit on the front step, seven-forty in the morning, and watch the sharp lights of Jupiter and Venus, brilliant and singular against the darkness. Joyce and Larry arrived last night on the way through to Kelowna. Second time in six weeks. Brodie disappears inside himself when his parents come. Joyce is in the kitchen, scraping up the last of her eggs and ketchup. The air so chilly, minus twelve degrees. I open the porch door and Skipper wriggles through, tears once around the yard, poops, and rips back in.

Where's the mustard? Joyce's head is in the fridge. Don't you guys keep mustard? Rice crackers, lettuce, mayonnaise, pickle jars strew the table.

It's too damn cold to go, Larry says, splashing skim milk on his porridge.

Well, Larry, Joyce says. In case you didn't notice, what this house needs is a little cheer.

Cripes, she says to the dog. Stand on your *own* feet, will you?

It's too damn cold, Larry says. Who wants to tramp around the mountains in the cold?

Joyce has been mad all morning. The doctor said her neighbour Grace Proproski died of lung cancer. She didn't die of lung cancer! She died of pneumonia. Caught it in the hospital too! Cripes! Joyce could've told them that! And now she's livid at the refrigerator delivery man who chipped a nick out of the wall when he wheeled their new fridge in six years ago. Don't they give these guys some kind of training? That's what I'd like to know! Can somebody give these lunkheads driving lessons?

I stand in my kitchen, reciting to myself the unread books that have found their way onto my shelves: *Motherhood and Mourning; The First Year of Life; The True Story of the Three Little Pigs; A Farewell to Childhood; Transformation through Birth; A Complete Guide to Achieving a Rewarding Birth; How Shall We Tell the Children?*

So I told him. I said, You want I should call up the manager? Is that what you want, fella? I tell you, that lit a fire under him.

I'm going to the hospital, I say. I swing on my coat and reach for the doorknob.

Now? Joyce whirls. Good God Almighty, it's seven-thirty in the bloody morning! Breakfast hasn't even settled. What's a few hours? She's not going to run away.

At the hospital, a mother exits the gown room, crying. She isn't coming back! She's had it. *Blessed are they who mourn.* I won't become attached! she sobs. A child herself, no more than eighteen, her yellow hair spills down her back, her lipstick fierce.

You look after him, she hiccups to the startled nurses who stand in the open doorway. I'm not allowed to touch him anyway. I won't have my heart broken. I won't! This unit's like living inside a ventilator! the girl-child cries. You breathe for us. You do it all!

A crowd has congregated at the far end of the room. A redhead is standing, hand on a careless hip, surrounded by nurses, chatting excitedly.

She's keeping her food down?

She's gaining weight?

Her hair's grown back?

I lift my head, strain to hear above the machines.

You *have* to bring her in!

We'll see you at the Christmas party!

The woman stands regal among them, accepting their words as if praise is her due.

When at last she turns to go, nurses trail her to the door. The woman steps through the doorway with a final wave.

I follow. Excuse me.

The woman looks down at me.

I was just wondering — it sounded as if —

I took my kid home? The woman pops a Dentyne stick into her mouth, Well. I did. She eyes her teeth, her eyebrows in a tiny mirror extracted from a messy purse.

I've never met one. A mom who got her papers, passport, and checked out of this place. I can't imagine. Our eyes collide.

Can we have lunch? I say.

Maggie

Fact is, I only have hours, I say.

Don't we all, sighs LaFlèche. We sit at the window of the Heartland Café, this winner and me. This redheaded stranger. This woman with the ten-stroke. With the trump card. This woman who defied them all and marched her baby home. Brodie has taken his parents to the mountains. The aroma of bean soup steams the room. Beneath it, the scent of soaps and candles from the adjoining shop. I stare at my face reflected in the steamed-up window. Now that I have the woman here, I can't think what to say. I'd hoped to see the child, but she left her at her mom's. Teething. Screeches bloody murder. She's a pain in a restaurant too.

I go to court Monday. LaFlèche snaps a fingernail. Mace wants time-sharing with the dog. Baxter's *my* dog.

A woman says earnestly at the adjoining table, Denial is a form of protection.

I twist to peer at her. That's what they say. They say that at the hospital. How did you do it? I ask LaFlèche.

Mag, mind if I call you that? I'll be frank. LaFlèche digs

muffin from between her braces. It isn't pretty. We're not talking the Gerber baby dying.

I squash a crumb. But you didn't lose — I haven't —

LaFlèche flaps a hand and flops back in her chair. Dead easy. Two-step program. One. Say fuck off to the doctors, and Two. Cart your kid home.

It's as easy as that? And she's doing all right?

Eats like a lumberjack. Melissa's fine. For Christ's sake, hospitals *carry* disease. Once you're in, you're up shit creek. Events escalate, Mag, until you're one, LaFlèche makes quotation marks in air, *of those!* Suddenly a woman blames any occurrence in the next thirty years on having lost that baby. I gained weight. You know it all started when I lost that baby. I lost interest in my job when I lost the baby. In the end we lost the house, you know. Spent all our money on the baby. Lost. Lost, LaFlèche waves a muffin, I turned lazy, fat, dull, I had no business sense. Maggie, I know you're skinny. I'm just saying. Losers. You're on that road. I need to clean my cupboards. Do you want your fortune told?

People keep opening the door. I'm getting chilled.

LaFlèche takes another bite, says, I swing open a cupboard door to grab a can of soup and everything spills out. The mess'll kill me. It was me who named him Baxter. Melissa? Gained three pounds. She's eating like a pig. LaFlèche tips her wrist. Got to skedaddle, honeybunch. Mom goes to work at three.

I'm going back to the hospital this afternoon, I say.

I tell you, Mag? My mom named me LaFlèche cuz I was

conceived in the back seat of a Chevy II in the gravel pit outside LaFlèche, Saskatchewan. Mace used to call me Flesh. LaFlèche sucks cider up her straw. Did you know that dragonflies are promiscuous? Like totally.

You had slight scoliosis as a child, a doctor said once, fingers climbing my eleven-year-old spine.

Will it get worse?

The curvature is very small. You're lucky.

He said, You're lucky.

So Melissa's perfectly okay? She's perfectly okay?

She's hunky-dory. Fat. She has three teeth. Forgets she ever saw a hospital. LaFlèche is heading back to the counter for a raspberry yogurt muffin to go. She holds up two red-pimpled ones. I signal no.

Right, whatever, LaFlèche calls.

She bursts back to the table, undoes her coat, dabs butter, talks lawyers and dogs.

…was drowning, Maggie, LaFlèche smudges pink crumbs. Both marriages. Suffocating. I was, she leans forward, pale-lipped, I was breathing water. LaFlèche crumples her napkin, rises.

I say, My cupboards are in order. It's my in-laws that need organizing.

If I was on Prozac, LaFlèche throws her scarf over her shoulder, maybe I'd like my job. Did you see the fire on Brisbois? A laundromat. Hell, fire, Maggie. I need fire. She takes a long last drag of apple cider, head thrown back. Baby, I need flames.

Maggie

I take the bus home from the Heartland Café. Poetry scrawls its walls. Chinook wind. The river's melting. *Ask anything in My name and I will grant it.* I float the two blocks from the bus stop to our little yellow house. I've wasted all the salt water I am going to waste. A light-filled day. See-through to the sky. Kalila's lungs are breathing without fifty per cent oxygen. It's down to twenty-three per cent. The doctor says that she could catch up to her enlarged heart. And her *right* kidney's fine. Women with only one kidney have been known to give birth. I can live with scars, can live with a child who may have to sit out phys ed.

I let the dog into the yard, but soon he's back, scratching at the door. There's so much heaven. It's not so far away. I pick up the morning paper, arrested by page three. An article advertising a faith healer, in town for seven shows. A week of miracles, the paper fairly shouts. My heart does one big flip-flop.

Something's stuck to my shoe. I look down. Skipper has dragged in a sea of leaves and a bloody pawprint. Cut on the ice. I am tending his foot when Brodie walks in the door. As he bends to untie his shoes, light catches the small scar on his forehead. When he was a kid, he barked at a neighbour's dog, who jumped and bit him. One childhood event Brodie remembers. His past, for the most part, has forgotten him. When we first married, I would find Brodie's notes scribbled to himself around the house.

> *The measured acceleration of the picket fence was 10.4 mls. Could the picket fence have fallen from an angle, causing the readings to be off?*
> *Early model of the universe — a sphere with holes in it that light shone through. The fundamental elements — earth, air, fire, water, not counting celestial —*

Brodie! I hold up the loosened sheets of the morning paper. There's a faith healer in town!

Brodie

You set your physics labs on the table and look at Maggie clutching the newspaper like news could save the world.

You try to formulate an imaginative position. Your imagination can't take you that far. You pick up Skipper's foot, he yelps but shakes a paw.

He was chasing the neighbour's cat, says Maggie. Ripped a toenail on the ice. The radio is crooning, something about a rubber ball and everything turning out okay.

66 CFR is giving away free tickets, Brodie.

You hold the bloodied paw, dab with a paper towel.

Brodie.

Don't be silly, Maggie, you say gently. Faith healers are con men. Bogus. Maggie has a way that makes the absurd seem plausible. You disappear into the bathroom and return with a cold wet washcloth, blood flecking your hands.

Brodie, you've always said, even scientists know that there is power in unexplained phenomena.

Scientists know nothing of the kind. Now that she comes

out and says it, it just sounds foolish. Was your day okay? You lean over Skipper's paw. Did you go to the hospital? It comes to you that you are craving licorice.

Brodie! I'd do anything for her.

You go tight-lipped. It's hogwash. The doctors will bring her round. You feel your our-child-is-secure-in-the-service-of-medical-science face. Your hands sudden and light against Maggie's hair. Touching her, you think with sharp-edged longing of the women at the school who chat about unimportant things: haircuts and cruises, meat loaf and buns for supper, the latest movies, the opera, closets to be cleaned.

Skipper, finding himself *not* the centre of attention, whines. Sits on his haunches in the beg position. Barks, though no one suggested he speak. Extends a hopeful paw, though no one said shake. Whips over in a jaunty roll, though no one has said, Play dead! He scrambles to his feet, looking expectant and happy.

A memory. You were ten when your rabbit gave birth to five babies. The rabbit lived on lettuce and carrots, but the day after the birth, you brought her oatmeal: a festive brunch for achieving Motherhood. You came home from school that night and she was dead. Diarrhea. Pooped herself to death.

That's when you lost what little faith you had.

You lay the washcloth against the pad of Skipper's foot. Okay, Skip. Skip! Shake a paw! Skipper flaps his paw, whining delight, and licks your hands, grateful once more.

Let me take you out for dinner tonight. You feel you owe

her something, but no. Maggie doesn't want to step into that world. So you make Pan. She sets the table while you fry two slices of bread, turn them over, break an egg on each and scramble, careful to keep the runny mixture safe atop each slice. Maggie slices tomatoes. You salt and pepper the eggs. The refrigerator motor cuts in.

Maggie's silence.

Maggie

I long to race out, start the car, drive to the hospital, kidnap my baby, escape on a healing pilgrimage to Lake Manitou. Brodie pours himself some milk, me water. My head bobs in the seaweed slap of Lake Manitou's waves. Manitou. Saskatchewan's saltwater lake. Saltier than the Dead Sea. A lake with magical powers. Manitou, which means intelligent, mysterious, invisible, and whole. The lightning storms that lit the lake, a hundred disparate zigzags, beckoning, signalling one another, me a child, crowded with my sisters at our summer cabin door, sweaters peeled off, shivering skin inviting the moist chill air, clutching each other at every thunder clap. Needles of rain stabbing the bent plants.

Rain's a miracle, our father said.

Ask anything in My name.

When I was a child people came from across the province, even from the United States, to immerse themselves in Lake Manitou's healing waters, cure their skin sores, arthritis, aching muscles, warts. Summer Bible Camp at Manitou Beach. Each morning we herded up the camp house steps, lustily belting, *Onward Christian so-old-iers, marching as to war…* We coloured pictures of Jesus gathered with his disciples at the seashore, pasted pictures of Jesus healing the sick into our Bible school booklets, the glue rolling into terrific balls that begged to be chucked against walls, stuck in one another's hair. Afternoons, we swam in the lake's cold waves, wrapped in green seaweed, eyes stinging, buoyed up to the surface by supernatural salt. When we read the story of Jesus walking on the water, Dougie Staganofski, at church camp to get out of doing dishes, said, I'll bet Jesus walked on *salt* water. That's all. Right then and there I stroked him off my potential-husband list. Trust a Catholic. Relying on works. No faith.

But Brodie is another story. He's a lapsed United Churcher. This is worse. Lapsed United Churchers don't count on faith *or* works to get them into God's good graces. United Churchers count on themselves; they count on order in the world; they count on natural science.

Brodie scrapes back his chair, disappears into the kitchen, and brings out my mom's home-canned pears. I spoon fruit into the cut glass fruit dish. The wind in the branches tonight sounds like an Aeolian harp. My father had one. Who knows where it is. Gone with the wind, my father said of things that disappeared. An instrument sounded by natural wind. David in the Bible had an Aeolian harp, sounded by the breath of God.

Brodie rises to make tea.

Samuel Coleridge said the harp was a tragic sounding of the experience of mankind. Dad quoted Coleridge: *It pours such sweet upbraiding... Such a soft floating witchery of sound... A light in sound, A sound-like power in light.*

What confounded me as a child was that the harp would sing its soft hum only when it chose, as if it had a mind. My father's harp wouldn't, for instance, show off on demand when my friends came to play. He laughed as my girlfriends and I gathered, breathless, in the open window.

Nothing tragic's happened, my father would say. No story to sing today.

One winter morning, I ran in from play, gasping that the power line had started an eerie bounce of its own accord. No wind. A ghost is shaking it! I cried.

That frost-thickened line is acting as an Aeolian harp, my father explained, drawing me against his rough overalls. Even wires and clotheslines sing, inspired by a tiny breath of air.

I look at the scattered pages of the morning paper on the table. People saved from plane crashes, birth mothers finding their adopted children, explosives refusing to go off, drowning victims revived, harps bursting into song. Miracles are everywhere. *Ask anything in My Name.*

Heal my baby. We do the dishes. Somewhere in the darkness a dog barks. Skipper answers, a nervous whine.

Just take God's hand
Look how a star hangs in His firmament
Look at a praising lark's ascent
Yes, God is here
Just take God's hand,
Look on a crocus thrusting through spring snow
Look o'er the sea tide's etching ebb and flow
Yes, God is here…

Inexplicably, Brodie pulls me, hands still wet, against his flannel shirt. A Brodie moment. Relying on silence.

Maggie

I'm at the front door in my nightgown retrieving the morning paper when I look up and there is my sister Rose. Rose! Whatever are you doing here?

There she stands, eight o'clock on a Monday morning with sponges and mops and disinfectant in a pail. Flew in last night. I'm bunking at Marigold's. I'm here to do winter cleaning.

Winter cleaning? Whose?

Yours.

Rose! Who does winter cleaning?

Maggie. You won't have done fall.

This is what my sister offers grief. Rose steps through the door and peers under my couch. Maggie. You can't just let things go.

Rose is a cheerful thump and slap of mop and soapsuds, window cleaner and rug shampoo. When did I last vacuum? I plunk myself on the ottoman, shame twisting my esophagus. Maggie Watson. The lazy, spoiled baby her sisters always said she was. Shoving her way to the front of the line. Me first! I want my baby whole.

What a hog! The other parents are settling nicely for parts. Missing kidney. No brain. No anus. Who do you think you are?

Rose sings as she dusts down the door frames. I grab my coat and head into winter. Skipper bounds ahead of me, shovelling a path with his nose. Netted snowflakes sashay to the ground. Metal scrapes cement, a boy in a Dr. Seuss toque shovelling our neighbour's walk. Skipper barks and leaps at each mouthful of snow. I plough through snowdrifts. Maybe faith is nothing more than works. Could I, could all mothers perform for better service? Tie back our hair in ponytails? Tie our yellow gowns mid-thigh. Positions, ladies. A-one and a-two and a-one two three.

> *Big bottle of pop and a big banana*
> *We're the gals from Louisiana*
> *That's a lie and that's a bluff*
> *We're from Neonatal! That's enough!*

What is faith if not yearning for reward for those who act? Let's teach those babies to demand their rights.

> *Set 'em right! Stamp stamp stamp clap clap stamp*
> *stamp*

Fight tonight! Stamp stamp stamp clap clap stamp
   stamp
We can score! Stamp stamp stamp clap clap stamp
   stamp
Little more! Stamp stamp stamp clap clap stamp
   stamp

By the time I've circled the neighbourhood, Dr. Seuss-hat-boy has finished shovelling a second driveway. He waves. Somewhere a siren wails. The boy bangs the shovel against the doorstep and rings the doorbell to collect his pay. He's still standing there in cement-shadowed dusk when I thump inside.

How do I find the shape of faith? Something to count on?

Brodie

You drive to the hospital after supper, leaving Skipper, restless, whining in the closed-in porch. Step into Neonatal ICU imagining the moon broken by trees, rain-drenched November sky, the sheen of silver ice, to find your child awake. So rare in this place of organized air. You sit down so the impassioned parts of you do not move on, through, out the window, back into rain and wind and moving objects. You reach for that little hand.

+

Sometimes the little princess gazed out across the landscape and imagined that all the little glass castles housed her own big family. Brothers and sisters, all hers, spilling down the hill. Sometimes their small sounds reached her ears: a cry, a cough, a shifting in a cot. On rare occasions The Sorcerer would appear in a great white cloak. Then he would poke and prod the little princess. Sometimes he brought other Sorcerers and they stood around her glass castle and talked and argued, as if she were the star of a great drama unfolding beyond her walls, and her observers could not agree on which part she should play. On these days, long into the afternoon, the little princess watched The Sorcerers touring the castles dotting the countryside, pausing to debate at each one, though never conferring with those inside.

Oh, how the little princess longed to venture out into the world beyond the hill of castles.

Maggie

A stiff north wind blows me through the parking lot, Foothills Hospital rising against a barren landscape. I have the urge to march around the fortress seven times, like Joshua did Jericho, singing "The Song of the Captives," and the walls will come tumbling down. A strange mélange of patients cowers against the building, smoking. Two clutch their intravenous poles as though the wind might lift them, a woman with a broken foot, grounded by her cast, two bundles in wheelchairs wrapped against the wind. They stare, flicking their cigarettes and their heads, like horses, to sail the smoke away.

I plunge in the door. The foyer cold. Take a breath to prepare myself for Dr. Martens, Dr. Vanioc, Dr. Whoever. Dr. Norton, whose eyes filled with tears the few times she spoke with me, quit two weeks ago. She wasn't cut out for this, a nurse said. She left to write a book.

We're still trying to understand what the baby's problems entail, the doctors say, shifting from foot to foot.

It's too early to tell.

It's only been a week, ten days, a month, six weeks, ten weeks.

Isn't this their *job?*

I take the elevator to the fifth floor, ride it with a man and a sullen child who glowers and sucks his thumb. On the fourth floor, the two exit, the child wailing, Are they gonna hafta kill me?

No one in the scrub room this morning.

I step into the hum of motors and activity. Dr. Vanioc and a doctor I don't recognize step out. They hold the door open for a mother. First-timer. No eye contact. Lowered head. Stunned. Like a caught criminal entering the light of jail. *I don't belong here!* No words, no parole. I have the urge to slap the woman's bottom. You're IT. Run! You're the loser! The way Winnie Peters used to flee the classroom hyperventilating, and hide in the bathroom, her mind a dyslexic nightmare, trying to straighten out the letters of a spelling quiz.

Na na. You birthed a preemie. The power of a label.

Lately life-away-from-the-hospital is a tie for moments of hospital life. Friends, mere acquaintances trying for really nice. Their gusty breaths, their strapped-on smiley faces.

Good thing she's just a baby. If she goes, you won't have had her long enough to get *too* attached.

I bet you'll be glad when *this* is over. As if *this* is a minor irritation, like a traffic tie-up.

We're praying. Though we're not sure what to pray for.

Well, we sure wish we could have seen her. Past tense. *Too late now.*

Does your baby make strange?

Ha. No, she reaches out. She *loves* the needle stabs, the hole chopped in her stomach, oozing fluid that shouldn't ooze, the tube stuck up her nose, another jammed down her throat. Tough love. You know? Just part of growing up.

I wind through the crowded aisles, past ragged babies with taped-up noses, tubes disappearing in and out of openings, arms bound against chests, arms flung over heads. So much laboured breathing. Babies on their backs. On stomachs. Drawn knees. Furrowed foreheads. Their old-man faces. Bee. Beebeebee. Their lives played out to their beeper soundtracks. I imagine all these babies crying, Mom! how heads would turn, pass a new dad holding his baby. The baby's tongue darts from between his lips, as if testing his environment, or trying to escape. His palms and the soles of his feet are purplish. The dad slides off his wedding band and slips it on the hand. The baby's whole fist fits within it.

Down's syndrome, one nurse says, low, to another, nodding. Came in last night. You learn to read the signs.

Down's syndrome! Someone found a name!

Skipper threw up on the floor this morning. Regarded me drearily. Turned and sat humped, back to me, while I cleaned it up. He's mourning the days when each sunrise held promise of a romp on Nose Hill. A dad sits holding a baby in the oak rocking chair against the far wall, an orange braided rug beneath his feet. He's staring into space, seeing another landscape. A row over, a mom arranges a tape recorder inside an isolette. The parents here don't talk much. What is there to say?

Just finished chest physio.

I turn toward the cheerful voice, a young nurse tripping over a cord. She grins and lays it against a neighbouring isolette. I haven't seen this one before. Gangly, a little klutzy. Maybe twenty-five. She holds in her hand a yellow toothbrush. I hold my dictionary. Face off.

Are you by chance Jewish?

Behind me, two nurses argue about the colour of Smarties. No, says one, the brown ones taste the same.

Excuse me?

The doctors were wondering if you might be Jewish.

I look at her.

DiGeorge syndrome. No Jews in your family history? DiRiley syndrome? Your husband's?

Sure, I'll be Jewish. Don't we all stem from Adam? I have a drop of Jewish blood.

We're going to repeat her blood gases shortly.

Is she worse?

She tolerated physio. The nurse waves the toothbrush. But she's had dusky spells. Temp's down. Of course, we don't have the whole picture.

Of course.

The nurse walks to another baby, scours the wee chest with a bright red toothbrush.

I glance down at the chart lying open on Kalila's isolette.

> Ask Dr. Hindle to evaluate exotropia.
> Obtain nerve condition studies
> Book for EXS
> Attempts to start scalp IV unsuccessful. Problems
>   with IVs going interstitial.
> Angiocath started by resident. Interstitial. IV
>   finally started in left hand.

The nurse returns to primly close the chart.

I slide onto the stool. What's this? A toque. Kalila, usually naked except for a diaper, is in a tiny white hospital gown, the kind that opens at the back, ties up the neck. Her huge blue diaper sticks out beneath it. And on her head, a blue-grey knitted toque. The kind a grandma would knit for a doll. It sits high, bending her ears. Matching her colour, dusky blue. She's breathing fast, as if air were being pumped in and out of her. Her stomach balloons, drops, balloons. A cut on her left foot. Blue bruising up the ankle. Her hand swathed in bandages, a needle stuck in, cardboard taped awkwardly round to hold it steady. Can't take my eyes off that little toque.

Who gave her this?

Her temperature was down, Mrs. Solantz. She wasn't warm. Somewhere down the line a beeper sings.

Could I wash her nighties? Who gave her this?

The hospital does that, honey.

I insert my hands through the thick plastic isolette holes. Knee against the cold blue metal drawer. Kalila breathes. I take hold of the unbandaged hand. Stroke, and the baby's fingers curl.

> *Baby's bed's a silver moon*
> *Sailing o'er the sky*
> *Sailing over the sea of sleep*
> *While the stars float by...*

Another mom seats herself by her baby at the far end of the room. Between us a long, untidy row of metallic boxes. Two doors at the bottom, an attempt at a dresser, dials and buttons cross the centre, made of steel. Babies perch in their top bunks, their lookout towers. Do the babies think this is an extended pyjama party? The glass, punctured with two armholes filled with plastic whorls to stuff a parent's love through. I look down past the rows of isolettes to a dad who has lifted the glass lid of his baby's tiny room and pulled out the shelf on which the child rests, the way he'd open an oven door and pull out the metal rack holding a tray of chocolate cookies. We are parents; we should be exchanging recipes, hollering down the aisles.

Hey! Could you bring me your Pork Medallions in Dijon Mustard Sauce?

Want to try my Chocolate Marbled Cheesecake?

The huge baby two rows over squawks. Works himself up, the big one with the voice. I get a sudden picture of baby Jesus throwing a tantrum. Glaring balefully at the lady hired to sweep out the hut. Jesus gumming dates and figs. Baby Jesus playing in the dirt of the cedar grove. *And she brought forth her firstborn son and wrapped him in swaddling clothes and laid him in a manger...* Hey, God, how come you got to have a healthy child? How come your kid got to live till thirty-three?

Silence, except for a nurse zooming the aisles, crying, Baby Schmidt's temp's up. Can you open the isolette? Take off a blanket. Oh, oh. Baby Minor's got loose stools. Yeah, greasy. Yellow. Better hold the MCT oil. Can someone call the cath lab for Baby Landonell's results? Medicine forced down, tubes inserted, blood let.

I rest my head against the glass. My right hand, if I reach, can just touch the paper skin; above it, the toque's prickly softness. Must be real wool. Kalila could be allergic. I want to warn my daughter, Don't accept gifts from strangers. Good lord, I forgot to hospital-proof my child!

No yanking out of each other's catheters.

No playing with needles.

No food tube fights.

No accepting toques from strangers.

The glass is cool against my forehead. Outside the window, snow falls. *Since you came, baby, the weather hasn't stopped.*

I close my eyes to the silent drop of icy snowflakes. Take this blue baby and lay her out in snow, dust her into a blue-shadowed little girl wearing a grey unbuttoned coat, blue leotards, a dusky grey-blue toque. The child breathes peppermint air, sinks against the crispy crust, swings her arms in arcs, scissors her legs. Sshhish, Sshhish. Toque dark against the diamond glitter. The child's cheeks shine ruddy in the snow light. She calls, laughing, Mommy, I a angel, Mommy, I a star.

I open my eyes. Kalila is flailing her arms and blowing mucus. The nurse rushes over, occupying my space. The red musical apple in the isolette's corner sings at the baby's kicks. The nurse shoves in capable arms, siphons the suction tube up the baby's nose, draws out endless amounts of thick green mucus.

Has Dr. Byars contacted you?

Who's Dr. Byars?

I long for home, for a familiar language.

The nurse says, He'll talk to you. Snakes out the sticky tube.

Stories are meant to lead somewhere. To rising action. Climax. Closure. And they lived Happily Ever After. From its beginning, Kalila's story, like a woollen toque, unravelling.

What's wrong? I make myself say, but the words stay in my head. The nurse repositions the hose, shoves it down the other nostril. The baby jerks, hoarse breathing, dry, in harsh fluorescent light. When the nurse finishes, she raises the little bed within the isolette to a forty-five-degree angle. The baby makes a bubbly sound.

He'll contact you.

The little pasty grey-white face grows slowly pinker.

Is she worse? I want to hold her.

Honey, she's tired now.

I want to hold her.

The baby lies lifeless with exhaustion.

She'll sleep if I hold her. She always sleeps better if I hold her.

> *Sing your way home at the close of the day.*
> *Sing your way home, drive the shadows away.*

11:42 a.m. Babe received in mother's arms.

$$\frac{\partial}{\partial \dot{q}_i}$$

$$i = 1, 2, \ldots, n$$

$$T - V, \quad T = \frac{1}{2} \sum_{i=1}^{n} m_i \dot{q}_i^2$$

$$\sum_i p_i \dot{q}_i - L \quad \text{where} \quad p_i = \frac{\partial L}{\partial \dot{q}_i}$$

$$\frac{\partial H}{\partial p_i}, \quad \dot{p}_i = -\frac{\partial H}{\partial q_i}$$

four

The Poisson bracket of two variables u, v

Deflection

$$[u, v] = \sum_k \left[\frac{\partial u}{\partial q_k} \frac{\partial v}{\partial p_k} - \frac{\partial u}{\partial p_k} \frac{\partial v}{\partial q_k} \right]$$

Then $\dfrac{du}{dt} = [u, H] + \dfrac{\partial u}{\partial t}$

Then $\dfrac{du}{dt} = [u, H] + \dfrac{\partial u}{\partial t}$

$$B = 0 \qquad \nabla \times \vec{E} + \frac{1}{c}\frac{\partial \vec{B}}{\partial t} = 0$$

$$\nabla \cdot \vec{D} = 4\pi \rho \qquad \nabla \times \vec{H} - \frac{1}{c}\frac{\partial \vec{D}}{\partial t} = \frac{4\pi}{c}\vec{J}$$

where $\vec{E}$ = electric field, $\vec{B}$ = magnetic field

and $\vec{D} = \vec{E} + 4\pi \vec{P}, \quad \vec{H} = \vec{B} - 4\pi \vec{M}$

$$\nabla \cdot \vec{B} = 0 \qquad \nabla \times \vec{E} + \frac{1}{c}\frac{\partial \vec{B}}{\partial t} = 0$$

$$\nabla \cdot \vec{E} = 0 \qquad \nabla \times \vec{B} - \frac{1}{c}\frac{\partial \vec{E}}{\partial t} = 0$$

Maggie

I hold the book I've picked at random off my bookshelf. Close my eyes. Picture my mother, reading with her finger, like a child after all these years. She can read at most an hour, then the page blurs. The doctors tell her macular degeneration is a mysterious disease. No one knows why an eye's blood vessels break and leak. Lately she has trouble recognizing faces. She tells people mostly by their shapes these days, their walk, their smell, their voices. Their outline is a blur. I can't make eye contact, she tells me over the phone. There are times I know I appear rude. I feel such shame.

On her last visit, Dr. Nichols jovially told her that in mythology, blindness is linked to inner sight. Birds see better than humans. My mother reading up on sight as she loses her own. Pigeons, for instance, see polarized light that is absent to the human eye. These same birds can be trained to pick out letters of the alphabet, a skill my mom is losing. A spindrift of sunlight at the window. My book slips from my knee. How I long for my mother's faith. Mine fell away somewhere. I listen to the prayer my mother will be praying. *Our Kind Loving Heavenly Father, Ye who said your kingdom is likened unto a child, Ye who said to the nobleman, Go thy way, thy child liveth, Ye who said, Suffer the little children to come unto me. Ye who sees the sparrow fall, Attend to the suffering of little Kalila.* I squint at a breath of sunlight shifting against the windowpane.

Maggie

A sunny Tuesday morning. I find myself standing in the fresh produce aisle. Shoppers negotiate carts about me.

Maggie Watson! I turn in the act of picking up a mango. Remember too late the touch of its skin blisters my own. Standing at the far end of the aisle is a woman I worked with at the seniors' complex. Bernice stands large in her overcoat, open, revealing a fuchsia paisley dress. Her feet, stuck in serviceable white nursing shoes, squeak my way.

So, Bernice says.

Umm, Bernice says.

I pick up three pomegranates, pack them in my cart. How's life at Confederation Lodge?

Things could be worse. Bernice pinches the kiwi. I moved to days. Remember Vivian? She worked in foods? She's developed a tremor in her left hand. Mm-hmm.

I set in my cart arugula, a bag of kale. Bernice goes for the romaine lettuce, leans close. Pear perfume. Who'd want to smell like fruit?

Bernice says, May be cerebral palsy. Vivian, she adds to my blank look. Oh, Bernice says, and Madge Middleton finally died. She snaps her fingers. Went just like that at Tuesday Bingo. It was so distressing for the others. And Ruth Barker, the activity coordinator — was she there before? — well, she took Velma's job — anyway, she didn't notice Madge had passed on, and kept shouting, Under the B-52! Under the O-12! Madge passed on in her folding chair beside old Julian Bates, who got so agitated when he noticed her gone, he hollered, Bingo! And Nattie Schue slid all the buttons off her cards. Was there a to-do when Nattie found she was out of the game for nothing! When all the excitement died, and the paramedics left, they had to start the game over on account of Nattie Schue.

I walk into morning light, pushing a cart of groceries I don't need: mangoes, shrimp, Chinese cabbage, lemongrass, leeks, a clump of beets. As I pull onto Sarcee Trail, window rolled down, the Rocky Mountains, the whole Bow Valley corridor, bursts into view in all its granite snow-topped sunlit splendour.

A chinook wind sings.

The world is turning on its axis.

Anything can happen.

Brodie

Hand in your quiz. I trust it's jolted you awake. Surprises are stimulating. Keep you on your toes. Harvey, you already wrote the thing. What's the point of complaining now? Take out your notebooks. Fifteen minutes left. No. There's no such thing in my class as free time. Chaos theory. With whom did it begin?

Mutterings. Scramblings. A frantic search for pencils.

Edward Lorenz, sir.

Early morning light streams through the classroom windows. Dust hangs, pale and shifting, students' faces hard to see.

Lorenz was fascinated by the unpredictable, the seemingly random behaviour occurring in a system that should be governed by deterministic laws. The kinds of systems Lorenz was dealing with were disordered, but Lorenz searched to find underlying order in his random data. To find such an equation, however, involves many variables. A very small initial difference may make an enormous change to the future state of a system.

Does this have something to do with butterflies? Frankie is combing his hair, holding a tiny hand mirror.

It does. And you look lovely, Frankie. The theory was first introduced to describe unpredictability in — Evan. Your toast popped.

And sure enough, the smell of toast wafts through the classroom. The students crane their disbelieving necks to find quiet Evan Stewart unplugging a pop-up toaster balanced on the radiator, and now he is pulling from his backpack a tiny tub of peanut butter, another of jam, and a plastic knife. Evan slathers his toast.

Sorry, Mr. Solantz, Evan says earnestly, mouth thick with peanut butter, but I practise on the swim team till eight-thirty Monday mornings and I don't have time for breakfast, which is, he waves his knife, according to Mrs. Mahovalich, my grade two teacher, the most important meal of the day. He cuts his toast in four, pops a quarter in his mouth. The kids are giggling — *now* they're wide awake.

Evan, be kind enough to give us a definition of the chaos theory.

Evan cheerfully stuffs in another quarter, waves a hand, pulls a baggie from his backpack, and drops the empty tubs inside, along with his plastic knife. He withdraws a napkin with a scruffy hen on it and wipes the grease from his desk. Swallows.

How weather around the world is affected when a butterfly in South America flutters its wings, sir, he says respectfully and cleans his teeth with his tongue.

You shake your head. Next time, Evan, it would be nice to share. Yes, Lorenz started with weather. And he found that the equations governing weather were so sensitive that he came to the conclusion that if a little butterfly palpitates its wings in one part of the world, it may affect the arrival of a hurricane or tropical storm — or divert it — somewhere around the globe.

Evan pops the toaster in his backpack, hollers, Ow! and dumps it back out to cool.

Right, you say. The chaos theory, which Evan is so aptly demonstrating here for us this morning, is a field of science that studies the complex and irregular behaviour of nature's systems, Evan being only one. What are some examples of the chaos theory in practice?

Hands bob the air.

The currents in oceans, sir.

The dripping of a tap.

The collision of billiard balls.

Russian roulette.

All correct, you say. Or let's take something closer to home. The evolution of the human species. Our body's inner workings. Even the human heart and its blood flow have a chaotic pattern. Or music. Not that many years ago a graduate student in electrical engineering at Massachusetts Institute of Technology used chaos theory to recreate musically variating themes in Beethoven's symphonies.

You sit down behind your desk. The twentieth century, grade elevens, is known for three monumental discoveries: relativity, quantum mechanics, and chaos theory. And who knows what new discoveries await?

I still don't get what a theory that can't be consistent gives us. Gurinder, polishing his glasses.

Hope, you say, standing abruptly. Such a system gives us hope.

The bell jangles. Chaos ensues, students slipping back into runners, stuffing textbooks into bags, and heading for the door.

Evan, you call to their departing backs, next week we review the big bang theory. We'll look forward to your demonstration.

Brodie

You walk through a windblown Sunday morning, weather
and light, smoky with early December, molecules hanging,
the wind's song snatched away. Then you open a door and
replace it with hospital clutter. A nurse is weighing Kalila's
diaper. You stand aside to watch the nurse's back, the way
her hair graces her slender shoulders, the tiny white scar on
her forearm you want to run a finger over, the muscles of her
upper arms flexing as she does her chores. When she finishes,
she smiles at you and you turn to your baby, watching the
way her small hand, lost in a baby dream, reaches out to
nothing, fist clenching, opening, clenching, as if latching on
to daylight.

The nurse says, Okay. Her creatinine level is high today.
One-ninety.

What should it be?

Forty.

Machinery chugs.

This means her kidney isn't functioning, not filtering the blood. The nurse taps the intravenous bag, looks back at you, a look that's almost coy. The baby's most comfortable this morning on her tummy. She turns to other duties. One side of Kalila's head is freshly shaved, what little hair grew back now gone, to clear a vein for another intravenous. The nurse returns to say they are administering a drug called Eprex — it makes red blood cells.

My father-in-law died Wednesday, the nurse confides, so I'm just back. Her hands sort out the cords. He had a heart attack, then kidney failure. Had he lived, he'd have been institutionalized. She has moved to stand next to you, gives you a sideways glance, then back turned to check the drip, she says in a careful, casual voice, My mother-in-law had to make the decision to pull the plug. She taps the tube above Kalila's isolette. It nearly killed her. She adds softly, She made the right one though.

You look at her sharply, but she has moved to arrange an isolette drawer. To fill the silence, to cover its startling implication, you pick up *The Little Prince,* take over the space beside the isolette.

> ...*seeds are invisible. They sleep deep in the heart*
> *of the earth's darkness, until some one among them*
> *is seized with the desire to awaken... It is such a*

secret place, the land of tears ... The stars are
beautiful, because of a flower that cannot be seen.

The baby's eyes are closed. You lean over her isolette, your cheek against its chill.

⁘

Little princess. Once upon a time Phoenician sailors had a shipwreck, and along with pieces of their wreckage, they washed ashore. Wet and bedraggled, they stumbled onto the sand and gathered together to see what they could salvage. One sailor retrieved a small cooking pot, another several blocks of natron, a chemical used most often for embalming the dead. They searched the shore for roots and seaweed, berries, gathered together sticks on which they piled the natron, and, after several tries, managed to light a fire. It soon grew into a bright blaze. The sailors shivered around its searing heat until their eyes grew heavy, and, one by one by one, the men slid into sleep.

Imagine their surprise when they awoke in dawn's first light. A hard and shiny decoration stuck to their cooking pot. They snatched up the pot. The decoration rode along. They all peered through. The sand beneath their fire had melted, run in a liquid stream, until it cooled and hardened into glass against the pot's rough surface.

Little princess, glass can awaken, melt, dissolve, glass can open a closed door —

You will your child this story.
You will her imagination.
You will her the energy to slip like an electron to
another level.

Brodie

Your heart whaps once, wham-whams erratically. You stare at the isolette, its small door flung ajar. Baby Leung's name tag untaped and dangling. What are the probabilities? A baby's fled his box.

An aide is housecleaning the tiny room, polishing the little chamber with a cotton cloth. The nurses, pinch-faced, don't look at one other, won't look at you. Hammering silence. Kalila opens her eyes, makes to cry. You offer your finger, and her little face moves back to serene. Brief cool caress of darkness in your hand. A baby. A life.

Here. Gone.

You sink down against your stool. Some people prepare against death their whole lives, edge through each day, heads cocked, the possibilities terrifying: hit by a car, gassed in your sleep, sliced by a mugger's knife. It's cold in here tonight. Backs turned in duty.

You watch small dramas stop and start. Plunged into this

hospital world, the catch of the neonatal door, the cadence of a nurse's heels, you don't know which is more unnerving, footsteps clicking toward you or the ones tapping away. You sit in the glare of the fluorescent lights. Kalila's eyes slip closed.

The doctors say they need time. What was Einstein's belief? *People ... who believe in physics, know that the distinction between past, present, and future is only a stubbornly persistent illusion. Time, as we understand it, does not exist.*

A flash of Joyce and Larry's living room wall: their three framed dead butterflies, stapled behind glass. You look at the spot where Baby Leung was held captive his short life. Hey, you want to say, let's start the experiment over. Nothing dies. You watch Kalila's puffing breaths. The particle collapses; it goes on existing as a wave. You watch your child's body stuffed with tubes and needles; memorize her blue and amber scars. You have sat back and waited for the moment of transfiguration. Water to ice. Mass to energy. Liquid to gas. Lead to gold.

A doctor enters ICU and speaks in a low tone to the resident in charge.

It's moving into winter. Dusk falls now before you eat your suppers, before you leave the house, move through darkening streets to the lights of Foothills Hospital, standing gargantuan against the sky.

The terrible desire to be wrong.

You think of Isaac Newton, detached from the world.

A secretive man, obsessive, driven by the mystic. He sought knowledge in all he came across.

He had a nervous breakdown.

A second doctor steps through the neonatal door. A scientist steps out, risks everything, walks an unchartered path.

Kalila jolts in sleep, flings out her arms. This daughter, the faintest pencil stroke of an equation. She's barely here. What holds her? Not medicine. Not science. You reach out to caress your small girl's blue-tinged forearm.

The moon has no light of its own, you tell your sleeping child. We can only see the moon because of its reflection off the sun. Your shadow baby stirs and sighs. You breathe with her, quick breaths flitting there, here, there, here.

+

Sometimes the little princess risked calling through her portholes. Hello? Hello? I'm here. I'm here. I'm here. And heads did turn. But mostly the wind snatched up her voice to echo off the hill. Played it against the other castles, boomeranged 'til it dissolved. A rustle of spirits. The princess glimpsed through an accordion of air, brome grass, sage, a tiger lily, salt-stung, sunlit. The white ones lifted their heads. Singing? No, only a chinook wind communing round the building. They turned back to their work. The little princess held her face against the glass, against bursts of erasure while the small ones' spirits gathered, sang her back. The little princess shone with anger and the place remembered her.

The light is thin in neonatal. You look up at the high windows framing squares of evening dusk. Imagine life outside these walls, imagine Kalila through these walls, the two of you escapees into an undulating landscape. Landscape. It makes you who you are. So it's your job to give her one. The soles of Kalila's pockmarked feet smelling of new-cut grass, Kalila and Skipper charging through wind and tearing rain, chaotic weather. Machines click on off on. What are the odds? You think of James Clerk Maxwell, whose research in the nineteenth century first drew attention to those specific systems in which the slightest uncertainty in their present state prevented researchers from accurately predicting their future state. You realize suddenly that by using Galileo's scientific process, science has created a world with few options. You can't make just one observation. You can't limit yourself to one reality.

You sit in the hum of chugging motors.

Imagine Schrödinger's box, lid flung aside.

Brodie

The day begins in raw fluorescent light and stays that way. You stand under the harsh bulb in the gown room, facing Dr. Vanioc, who, in a rare move, has seen you by the isolette and called you out. The doctor clears his throat. I — yes, wanted to chat. The baby's blue spells mean she hasn't been getting enough oxygen. Because of the hole in her heart.

Fix it.

We're at a bit of a stalemate. She's too sick to risk an operation. As a result of the oxygen deprivation, it is a possibility that she may be mentally retarded.

You try to get the words wrong.

But, then, of course, that's normal, considering all she's been through.

Who says the word *retarded*? Retarded is not normal.

The doctor looks past you through his spectacles. You could be in different galaxies.

The normal force is your favourite force, you've always told your students. Your weight is the force of gravity, so when you sit on a chair, for example, the force of gravity pulls down on you. And the chair pushes back up on you with a force called the normal force. Think of it as a reaction. Your chair actually knows if someone heavy or light is sitting in it, so it can gauge how much it should push back.

Push back.

You feel your own chaotic blood flow whamming against your eyes. Your child, neither dead nor alive, is being kept in a box. And no one is bothering —

The doctor shifts in his shoes and claps his hands, So, there it is. We're doing what we can.

They've not removed the lid.

We're trying to keep her comfortable.

They've made the choice not to imagine.

We're working to keep you informed…

They have made one kind of observation.

The doctor's voice is hearty… trying to deal with her problems straight on.

They have limited themselves to one reality. *Look sideways. Newton went blind from staring at the sun.*

The doctor's language thins to a cough. As if absolved, he leaves the room.

You watch him move through the doorway, leaving a sprinkle of aftershave. These doctors are the kind of men whose world turns on measure, on method, on statistics.

And what are they measuring for? What they think they already know: the probability that a child will not get well.

After a while you put on a hospital gown and slip your wrists under the stream of water.

Kalila lies in her isolette, bluish, eyes open.

A baby girl has all her eggs at birth, a nurse chats to another at a neighbouring isolette. She twists the top of a bag of clear liquid dripping into Baby Wong. Yes, and a baby leaves some of her X chromosomes behind in the mother's body when she's born. The nurses fiddle and adjust the numbers. A mother carries her child forever, the nurse says. Imagine that.

You imagine. You stare at the needle sinking into Baby Wong. On the neonatal floor, you spy a stone slipped from a purse or pocket, the bronze colour of spun gold, edges tinged brown; a tiger's eye. You retrieve it; fit it against your thumb. Isaac Newton and his search for the philosopher's stone. You look at the equipment that keeps your baby girl alive: oxygen tanks, apnea monitors, heart monitors, drip bags, respirators, oxygen dispensers, IVs, bilirubin bulbs, heaters. Blinking lights, flashing numbers, warnings of cardiac arrest. The stone warms against your fingertips. You look around at the exhausted babies, battling low birth weights, intrauterine growth retardation, respiratory distress, seizures, asphyxia, infections.

One day an armoured knight rode up the hill. He opened the door of a glass castle, reached out his hands to a small boy. The knight released him from his prison, seated him on his steed. They galloped toward the sky —

✢

You stand abruptly. The stone clatters to the floor. You walk out of neonatal, pulling out your cell.

Maggie, I'm coming to pick you up. Maggie. Let's go for a drive.

Dr. Vanioc

Sunday evening. Dr. Vanioc drives down Highway #1 toward Calgary, two hours of solitude, a tree every twenty kilometres, radio off, not harangued by anything or anybody. Still light low on the horizon. It was dark when he left the city Friday — heart shifting into first gear after months of splintered hammering, worries slipping like flow charts out the window, the dog keeping up an excited whine — and will be darker when he hits the outskirts tonight.

He fought rush hour for the silence of those hours alone in the truck, and now two more, no wife, no phone, no child, in his cammo cap that Diane says makes him look mental. Two nights at Murray's farm outside of Brooks. Two days tramping the bush, guns over-and-under, carried broken, the guys fanning out, Brad heading upstream, Cal crossing the beaver dam, Murray striding ahead, kicking at grass and thistles. One of the dogs going on point. An explosion of colour and wings. A shot cracking the air. The bird plummeting. Whit and Connor — Brad's dog — rushing in.

The fraternity he feels hunting is hard to express to Diane. Everything a question of how to explain to Diane. You have to trust people, that they won't shoot you. Diane thunks the iron against his best shirt and says she doesn't have to drive two and a half hours into the country and tramp through bush to find out her friends won't shoot her. You don't bring outsiders along without asking the others, Dr. Vanioc says lamely. This confirms for Diane that they're nothing but a sixth-grade clique. You don't let slip to other hunters where you hunt, he says. And if discovered, you certainly don't tell them how to work the area. Never show your cards.

Diane slaps the ironing board down, carries it to the closet, and gestures out the window. Why don't you just build a treehouse in the big maple, swing a few ropes, and have sleepovers in *our* yard, pound your chests, and play at being guys. Hunting has its own kind of order. He doesn't convince her. He never will.

Whit didn't run into a porcupine this year. Last November he disappeared on point. When the thing didn't fly, Whit attacked. Dr. Vanioc shot the beast in frustration and turned to his shrieking dog. Three held him down. Cal took the hind end, Murray the body, the owner gets the teeth. Brad yanked the quills out with the pliers someone always carries. No point putting off the pain.

Whit missed two birds this weekend, but Connor found them. Whit didn't even know, and Dr. Vanioc is glad for that. The dog was so wiped, he had to lift him up into the truck box when it was time to roll. He's snoring back there and once in a while he yelps in his sleep. Dr. Vanioc rubs his shoulder. The best time of the day is five to six-thirty. That's when they sit around in the dusk and dark and visit in the field before they shower and go out for dinner. Tell stories of the day, how Connor made that perfect retrieve, then last minute swam across the creek away from Brad and plucked the bird with his teeth, ate the entire thing, eyes fixed on Brad, checking out his reaction. Never did it before. Never will again. Everyone guffawing. Brad working his mouth and scowling.

Men only talk when they're doing something. Say things in the dark they wouldn't say in light. Brad's worried about his kid — the second — Cory — who can't settle down in junior high. Dr. Vanioc wonders if the boy's drinking. He's been friends with Brad and Murray and Cal for more than twenty years.

Dark light slips past his cracked-open window. He feels sad and good and everything's a question of perspective. There's order in the world and part of that order is death. The medical system has created the illusion in the city that every kid will live forever. He wipes his hand across his stubble. He can feel embedded dirt. The ritual of the hunt. Whit was bred for this. There is a strange companionship between man and dog and bird. Each knows its place. And for him? The going out and doing it is an attempt to forget. Forget Diane's cold frustration, forget the drugged infants fighting for breath.

Hunting teaches you that life is chance. There's a winner and a loser. That's just the way it is.

Dr. Vanioc looks in the rear-view mirror. He can see the top of Whit's crate. This may well be Whit's last year. The smartest dog he's ever had. He remembers so many years ago, Whit flushing out his first pheasant. He went on point, just a little bit of a thing, not yet a year, quivering, not even knowing what a pheasant was. He shook for two minutes after the whole thing was over, the bird flushed out and shot. He didn't know what had happened to him. Just stood there, trembling. Dr. Vanioc praised him and that little thing looked into his eyes, so full of a feeling he didn't understand. Dr. Vanioc feels a ripping in his rib cage. Why does this move him more than his own child's first steps? By instinct, that dog did everything perfectly the first time. Whit makes a snuffling sigh. It's sad to see the decline of a dog. And of the men puffing along. They're no longer twenty, any of them. Dr. Vanioc had his first child at thirty-nine. What was he thinking? Diane only thirty. It was money. No money until he specialized. Now he has no time. You feel time's passage, hunting. The ranchers' children grow up, start to tag along. Carry a gun for the first time. Dr. Vanioc looks out over the darkening prairie. All this landscape to move in, like an old familiar song. And the stories. All the stories of pheasants and kids and dogs. He stretches in his seat and listens to the tires hum.

Maggie

Here on the sunlit river path we climb, the outside air a sharp surprise, push into the flesh of the afternoon, into silence shoved by a ripping northeasterly, this outdoor room of wind.

Brodie pulls at my scarf, fixes it around my ears, turns up my collar, protecting me from weather. The clouds riotous above. A deer starts, bounds away, a red fox glides through the underbrush and disappears in a bend of trees.

When I open my eyes, Brodie and the world are back in view. Whipped bushes, bobbing branches, chilled grey sky. The deer appears over the crest, ready to bolt.

The water's lapping rushes. A woodpecker needles a sharp staccato against a fir. Everywhere, nature in song. A helicopter's rap-beat rises and recedes. Brodie enfolds me against his thick coat. What's this? Brodie is talking.

Voice muffled in my hair. Maggie, she isn't — the doctor says — she isn't getting better.

We look at each other, breathe in wood smoke, river water, the damp smell of the trees.

Cogs click into place.

There are four clocks in neonatal. No direction we can face without reminder. Time is ticking down.

A crazy possibility thrusts its head up on this windblown path.

Let's make a break.

The great escape.

Stop thinking. It only drives you crazy.

Stop thinking. Act instead.

The woodpecker hammers out an exclamation.

Dare we? Just cart her off?

Said aloud, the thought hovers, like quotation marks in air. Words cannot be undone.

If she stays, her days are numbered.

No baby could flourish in that atmosphere!

Damn it. Let's take charge.

The doctors have given up.

They rarely come to see her.

She scares them.

We can't stop looking at each other.

We can't sit back, wait for a happy ending.

Help won't come from the hills; you have to climb, find it yourself.

She's wasting away.

She needs parents.

She needs a home.

She's ours. She's ours to take!

There on the windswept path, the idea formulates.

Because a photon responds to a momentum experiment doesn't mean it has momentum. To these doctors, she will never be greater than the sum of her parts.

Hope opens like the glimpse of a surprise zipper in the folds of a pleated skirt. Hope, a lid screwed off a jar. A lid pitched off a box.

Brodie paces, wind pulling his hair. If a person desires certainty he has to create it himself. We'll create her future, Maggie! Brodie's face shines boyish, lines etched round his eyes these last few months erasing. The idea expands like light, rushing ahead. It will take concentration. It will take belief.

We have to believe the things that matter are going to survive.

Two wheels spin in two chests.

There is one choice.

Take Charge.

Brodie

You make your way, Mr. and Mrs. Solantz, into the small and stuffy side room. Maggie has the glow that luminesced her pregnancy, a fairy story blossoming within.

The doctors wait in a semicircle. One you've never seen. Mr. and Mrs. Solantz have requested this meeting. Highly irregular. Fingers tap. These are busy men. The clock reads 1:03.

Dr. Vanioc offers Maggie a chair, then you. Whatever the doctor puts in his hair, it holds its form. You sit. The doctors stand. The meeting begins.

Introductions. The new one's Dr. Fezner, the kidney specialist.

Yes, there are problems at the hospital, as at all hospitals, as in all institutions, Dr. Vanioc says.

True, no one is coordinating, the doctors nod, solicitous.

We're working in the direction of changing that, Dr. Byars says.

You feel those extra cups of morning coffee swooshing

to your heart. Maggie slides forward on her chair. We can't tell if she's getting better here. If we could have some kind of guarantee that she's not fallen between bureaucratic cracks.

Mrs. Solantz, we can't just...

Watson.

You clamp Maggie's hand. We simply cannot go on knowing there is nothing being done.

A pause. There is a lot of breathing.

The doctors confer: they feel bad about the situation. Yes, they're still attempting to find out what's wrong with the baby. She's not an easy case. No, they aren't just letting her vegetate.

Dr. Showalter glances at his watch. Well, we're here if you want to talk. You can always catch us individually.

We prefer not to push parents, chimes eager Dr. Fezner.

We wish we could tell you we could change this and this and this, says Dr. Summers.

Maggie stands. Her chair scrapes the brown linoleum. You rise with her. We want to take our daughter home.

A shocked and fragile silence trails on a fine silk thread. The doctors shift their eyes onto one another. All come to rest on you. They're men. They want you to acknowledge common ground. Separate yourself from your emotional wife.

This may not be the time, Dr. Vanioc says after a bit of throat clearing.

Oh, Lord. You got the time wrong.

Maggie squeezes against you, hair smelling of vanilla. We've talked this over. We've thought it through. We want to take her home.

More glances exchange.

It's just, we don't have the whole picture — Mr. Solantz — it may not be in the best interest —

Mistakes have been made, Dr. Vanioc takes over, carefully confident. Leaning on the passive tense. A position is needed. Dr. Summers spoke to Dr. Sinclair about the heart. There was a medical decision made not to operate.

And we weren't told?

It went back to the committee.

So many experts, working in isolation. Lungs. Kidney. Bones. Heart. Sinew. Pieces of baby.

What will be the next step to take her home?

Dr. Vanioc clears his throat. This is highly unprecedented — You should give it more thought. Only babies —

We have. That's why you're here.

How could I force the referring pediatrician to come in? Dr. Sinclair says with sudden and irrelevant intensity.

Everyone looks at him. You picture particles dissolving into waves that build and rush, bowling these perfect-postured doctors over. They're trying to keep the focus, keep things within their control. Well, there's not enough room for everyone on this stage. It's the doctors' turn to get off.

Dr. Vanioc says again, quite gently, Parents' memories depend on the final outcome. You must use common sense.

When has common sense been a reliable guide to understanding the universe? Light cracks the small window. We will take our daughter home.

Brodie

You have a field of view, you tell your grade ten science class in your sun-dappled winter classroom. The sounds of shouts and a smacked volleyball resonate from the gym. You can measure this field with a microscope.

The students gather their rulers and crowd in. The smell of teenagers. The smell of gum and salami sandwiches, sweat and hair gel.

We start off on low power, you say. This is magnified forty times. Put your rulers under your microscopes. Your students comply. See the millimetre lines? Your job is to determine your circle of vision. How many millimetres it is from one side of the circle to the other?

The students measure.

Now increase the power by ten times to four hundred. What's your field of vision compared to what it used to be?

One-tenth the size it was before.

What does this mean?

Your students look at you.

The more power you use — ?

— the more detailed the observation of your specimen.

The more power you have, the narrower your field of vision.

Exactly, you say. The more power you have, my friends, the less you see of the whole.

$$\frac{\partial H}{\partial q}$$

...bracket of two variables u and v

$$= \sum_k \left[\frac{\partial u}{\partial q_k} \frac{\partial v}{\partial p_k} - \frac{\partial u}{\partial p_k} \frac{\partial v}{\partial q_k} \right]$$

$$\frac{du}{dt} = [u, H] + \frac{\partial u}{\partial t}$$

$$\frac{du}{dt} = [u, H]$$

five

Superposition

$$\frac{1}{c} \frac{\partial \vec{B}}{\partial t} = 0$$

$$\vec{H} - \frac{1}{c} \frac{\partial \vec{D}}{\partial t} = \frac{4\pi}{c} \vec{J}$$

...ic field, $\vec{B}$ = magnetic field

$$\vec{H} = \vec{B} - 4\pi \vec{M}$$

$$\vec{E} + \frac{1}{c} \frac{\partial \vec{B}}{\partial t} = 0$$

$$\vec{B} - \frac{1}{c} \frac{\partial \vec{E}}{\partial t} = 0$$

$$\nabla^2 \vec{E} - \frac{1}{c^2} \frac{\partial^2 \vec{E}}{\partial t^2} = 0$$

$$\vec{E} = \vec{E}_0 \, e^{i(\vec{k} \cdot \vec{r} - \omega t)}$$

Maggie

A dinner invitation. *Dinah Engagement*, Brodie calls it. A British couple twice our age from church. We barely know them. A sympathy invite, clearly, but what the hell. They invited us months ago, again just before Christmas, though they hadn't in the four years we knew of them before Kalila's birth, so we politely and firmly turned them down. But suddenly, I'm up for anything. A chinook has blustered in this Friday afternoon, the air is heady, teasing, gusty, defying anybody not to feel flirtatious. Our first outing since Brodie's school dance. Celebration in the air. Children, pumped on the wind's energy, race, chasing caps, laughing, pushing each other down Calgary's melting streets. A chinook brings "miracle" into the realm of belief: There's a chinook out there. Anything can happen.

Brodie steps in the door as I'm slipping into my black brocade pants, a dark blue silk blouse, my blue-black sapphire earrings. Shit! I snag a cuticle on my blouse. It's palpable: something in the air that disallows unhappiness. An energy zapping between us that we can't ignore. Brodie takes my face in his hands, entangles himself against me, says, Maggie, you're so pretty.

My pants are too big.

Last Christmas, pre-pregnancy, these were new; now they hang across my hips. Just to verify this, Brodie sticks his hand down the front, says, Good Lord! So they are! I laugh, wiggle away. It's our Before Life. The one we were nonchalantly living when this one came along and whammed us broadside, knocking us onto another track, heading god knows where. But our world has shifted: it's veering back in the right direction.

What are their names again? Brodie asks.

Brodie! For God's sake! Irvin and Virginia. Try to remember!

Grinning, Brodie splashes cologne on his face. I know what he's thinking: Maggie's old voice, her irritated voice. Her the-worst-thing-in-my-life-right-now-is-your-lack-of-memory voice. Brodie hasn't a care. Virginia and Irvin. Irvin and Virginia. The baby's coming home! Brodie practises conversation openers. So I hear you British like to conquer. I slap his hand.

Half an hour later we spin out the door under a sky of rolled-back blue. Gusts whirl what little snow there is, scoop leaves from shining streets and hurl them at the car. Brodie has to grab tight to the steering wheel so we don't fishtail into oncoming traffic. I roll down the window; frenzied wind attacks my hair. I punch an oldie-goldies station. Rock and roll.

So here it is. So here we are. The house on Mission Road. We blow up the walk. The night begins with olives.

What do you do? the woman called Pearl asks me sternly. This second guest-couple, Pearl and Carl, are twenty years our senior too. Pearl has one eye that weeps, causing everything she says to vibrate with melodrama.

Well, I've just had a ba —

And *you?* She stares in the direction of the armchair Brodie's perched upon.

Brodie glances surreptitiously about, leans forward. I'm a physics teac —

We clean jails, Pearl snaps. All eyes point to this pinch-faced friend of Virginia's who sits straight-backed beside her tiny husband. Outside the chinook wind moans crankily.

We had this couple working for us, Pearl pauses. At the *jail.* She is wearing maroon ankle socks over her nylons.

Virginia bites into an olive.

The man had no interest in sex. *Poor* thing. Everyone takes this in. It's not clear which member of the aforesaid couple deserves the adjective.

Drat it! Virginia says. These are the wrong olives. The pit appears at her lip and disappears again behind her napkin. I ordered spicy. Of all the —! They sneaked me pungent!

But the idea of sex in a *jail* turned him on, Pearl slides forward on the sofa. This woman invented italics. Now what he didn't *realize* —

Sod it! While the owner sidetracked me tasting his linguine, his assistant wrapped inferior olives and slipped them in my bag!

Pearl shoves her red-ankled feet together. Opens her mouth, pops it closed.

I look from Virginia in her severe nut-brown dress to Pearl, who wears a shimmering taffeta, high ruffled neck, her legs have fallen open at the knee. Not only are the ankle socks astonishing in their redness, but they are trimmed with frilly pearled edges that furl outward, daffodil-like, and her shoes look 1940s, laces and an open toe.

The thing *is*, Pearl zings a look at Virginia, but Virginia just keeps chewing, there's a television monitor in *every* washroom. Mmm-hmm. You get the picture. So while they went at it, she flaps a hand to each in turn, ex-*cuse* my language, on the newly scrubbed bathroom floor, still *wet*, the *only* time, let me tell you, the wife could *get* it, she cranks her head, looks meaningfully at Carl, who gulps more gin, the guards ordered pizza, stood around at the station monitor, and *watch* —

Irvin clamps down Brodie's reaching hand and shrieks, Don't taste the olives!

Brodie shoots a fearful glance at Pearl. There is a lengthy

silence after which Virginia asks Pearl's husband to mix the drinks.

What will you have? Carl asks me. Carl looks like a jockey masquerading as a World War One RAF pilot. He has the lack of height, the bomber jacket, which he keeps on in the house. His cigarettes are tucked inside its pocket, hair slicked back, a little moustache. Tiny hands. Perhaps a bit of wine?

Yes, wine is nice, Virginia says, distractedly carting off the shameful olives. We'll have wine for dinner.

Mmm, gin?

I sip my gin and tonic. Try the crackers with herbed cheese. Dare not a glance at Brodie.

Where's the baby? Carl says.

Actually she's in the hosp —

Jadwiga Chmelyk's *dying!* Pearl hollers toward the kitchen.

Virginia returns and Carl replenishes the drinks. An argument ensues, a heated conversation in which the four try to outdo one another naming how many people they know who have dropped dead in the last year. Pearl pronounces hors d'oeuvres, *horsie doov-res*, causing Brodie to swallow his purloined olive whole. The list stretches competitively to Irvin's grandmother's sister's friend, Pearl's church caretaker, a golf partner, a ticket agent who served Virginia at Bass Outlet. Died of a bee sting. One.

Brodie takes the offer of a second vodka.

Dinner is artichoke hearts. Leg of lamb. Potato broisettes.

Gold plates, Pearl's little husband murmurs, tapping his own. He's on my right. He leans so close our arm hairs brush. Four-hundred-and-fifty dollars per cup and saucer, this set. He takes a demure sip of his wine, looking pleased.

Our cleaning lady keeps scraping away surfaces, Virginia announces. Irvin is dishing up each plate, handing them down the table. Virginia pauses, frowning, to watch him lop off a chunk of fat. We've had to hide our plates, our saucers.

Marishkya's also scrubbed off the surface of the ceramic tiles on the bathroom floor, more lamb? says Irvin.

No thanks, says Pearl. A bit tallowy for my liking.

Carl says, I shall.

A scathing stare from Pearl.

Marishkya rubbed the gold inlay off our antique chair. Virginia says in triumph, The woman can't stop cleaning!

We simply must get rid of her, says Irvin.

Eighty-six-point-five per cent silver, Carl whispers in my ear, brandishing a spoon, his breath a hot breeze across my neck. You have a good figure! He smells of stale smoke. Nineteen-twenties smoke. I look at the spoon in his hand. Check my fork. Ignore his comment. The silver collection is inscribed with a flourished *A*. Irvin's last name is Woolhouse. Did they steal the silver?

Electronic shutters, Irvin is saying with a wave of his hand. I have them fixed so they all close at one time. They're automatic. Virginia is jabbing buttons on the stereo.

I got quite a start when Irvin began courting me. Virginia, standing, planted in her shoes. The first time he swooped closed the shutters, I felt — her fingers flutter to her ample chest — seduced!

Brodie looks astonished, then very stern.

Darling, what's the name of that bridge in Vienna? Irvin asks. The one the groom carries the bride across for luck?

Some grooms have to carry their bride across *seven* bridges to get *any* luck, Pearl says. Women in Vienna can't afford scrawny husbands. She sniffs at Carl and turns away, tongue searching out a tooth.

Carl shoves a narrow thumb in Pearl's direction. She stepped out shopping for antiques in Vienna last summer, he murmurs, and showed up at the hotel three days later. He shrugs, reaches for a third helping of lamb.

I gingerly accept Virginia's offer of the four-hundred-and-fifty-dollar teacup.

Carl, ignoring the signal for dessert, and Pearl's pursed lips, saws off another chunk of meat with his eighty-six-point-five per cent silver knife. A clock strikes nine.

Irvin says, I've just repaired my clock. He lays down his knife and fork. Face wasn't there. Just the hands. They don't make things like they used to. It's a bloody nuisance. You expect the parts to work. I had to recut the gears. Hung weights on them finally, so the new gears would wear into each other. Ah, there go the blinds.

And sure enough, in one swoop, on all sides, the landscape

disappears and we are enclosed with four strangers, tea, and a dry European cake. Irvin offers liqueurs.

After dinner, Irvin ushers Brodie into his study to show off his pocket watch collection. Carl isn't invited, but then Carl's fifth glass of vodka has pinned him to his chair. With the alternative of being crushed under Carl's longing gazes while examining the bunions on Pearl's feet — she's due for surgery — and the stitches behind her ears — she's had a facelift — I trail along. There, in the back room, trapped under the coffee table glass, lie Irvin's watches.

Watches that date back to the eighteenth century, Irvin says. They glint dull gold and silver.

History under glass, he raps the table. Without watchbands, the watches look disabled. Irvin says, I can give you the history of each one. This one? Belonged to a French count. This? Early nineteenth-century Britain. This, a Jewish moneychanger. That one's a pedometer. It measures how far a person goes. Came out of the Spanish Civil War.

I point to one swathed in a tiny bag of grey brocade like a bunting bag. Could I have a peek at that one?

Absolutely not, says Irvin. They must be kept sterile. He taps the glassed-in tabletop again. Museum pieces. These babes have walked through history. Did you know, he adds, at the turn of the eighteenth century, watchmakers got together to try to regulate the ticking of all clocks?

What for? I ask.

Irvin swings on me. Why, to control time! Have you not studied Umberto Eco? Did you not know a heartbeat sets its rhythm to the ticking of a bedside clock? Irvin looks disapprovingly at Brodie's digital watch. Now, your watch there. It's useless. It shows no circle of time. It just records a moment — look: ten-forty-three. It has no face to harbour where time's gone. Or where it comes from.

Well, time is relative, says Brodie.

Irvin waves Brodie's comment away, his gesture takes in all his watches, All keep perfect time, and he launches into an explanation of the perils of insurance for watch collections. I manouevre for the salon door. Brodie grins at me. Great timing! I am treated to a peek behind Pearl's stitched-up ears.

More rounds of cake and tea. Carl is gently snoring. Pearl appears set on staying until time itself runs out; she's onto traffic on German autobahns and doesn't even wave goodbye when at half past eleven, we slip back into the night, giggling, holding each other up on the thin-iced sidewalk. The wind has died. Air balmy with chinook. The roads shine blackly wet.

Whew! Brodie chortles as we climb into the car. To think we turned down previous invitations!

We gun down Crowchild Trail, light-headed. The story has shifted gears.

Maggie

I breeze into Neonatal ICU on gusty winds of change. I want to hold her!

A nurse opens the glass lid that encloses Kalila. The baby's startled face against my breast.

A note taped to a nearby baby's isolette: *Allergy to soy. Attempts to pull out tube.*

Suicide Watch!

I picture babies flinging themselves in droves from their little bunks, babies stuffing squeaky rubber barbells down their throats, babies lying grimly on their food tubes. Not this baby. The bumpbump bumpbump of her heart. Kalila blinks cool air. I slip my hands beneath the baby's nightie, smooth hot skin. *Flesh of my flesh.* The baby shifts, stretches one foot. Ahhhhh.

We've tipped our toes into a fairy story; dreams do come true.

Brodie

Five-seventeen. You head home. Exams to mark. A sudden stab of grief, a sudden wrench of joy. You set your books down on the counter, watch a lone winter ant labour through a honey-stickied patch of counter.

A survivor.

Wind rushes your veins.

You are entering the unknown.

The future keeps on coming. They can't take that away.

Dr. Vanioc

Dr. Vanioc steps into the den to find that Diane has mounted a Colville print she bought online. It's hanging on the feature wall. He snaps open a beer, drops on the couch, puts up his tired feet. There's not much more than a moon and a cow. His head is aching. The cow is sleeping in a field. *The child's lungs aren't clear.* The sky has windblown clouds. *As long as you keep parameters sterile and artificial you are taking a chance.* The cow is in the foreground, *a different kind of chance,* a cattle shed on the horizon. *But then when has Dr. Vanioc taken a chance at all?* He squeezes the pain against his backbone. *The parents are right in how they've interpreted* — the cow's back gently contours, rhyming with the hills. *But in someone that small a judgment can be inaccurate* — Bill Vanioc drops his feet. This picture should be peaceful, pleasing — Diane!

Diane appears in the doorway with Cy and a plate of cheese and crackers. The baby, face smeared, grins, reaching for Dr. Vanioc. Isn't it nice? Diane goes on about the tonal contrasts. They make the earth more luminous than the moon; and so the picture feels enchanted. The baby grabs Dr. Vanioc's face. He doesn't feel enchanted. He feels exhausted, hypnotized. He's drinking his beer too fast and on an empty stomach. *If she asphyxiates* — his son's tiny fingernails scratch and scratch.

Dinner and *W5*. The plight of immigrants in our country. A cow dozes above Diane's onyx bowls set on a weathered sky-blue entry table. Reality has shifted. Overqualified for jobs.

Maggie

February 26. Thirty-three below. A play of light. Ice fog with sunny breaks. Rustle of snowfall.

Kalila's coming home.

One last time I step into the neonatal landscape. Survey the clutter, the thick black cords entangling, endless outlets clutching behind countless little beds. I have spent hours talking with the nurses, the doctors, the psychologist, the Upjohn organization who, like a big fat fairy godmother, will pay the bills. *Yes, we know it will be hard. Yes, we're grateful.* What do they want? Grovelling?

A baby carriage in the corner. An empty rocking chair. No abandoned glass slipper, no spinning wheel prick here. No poisoned apples. This fairy tale will have a happy ending.

Baby Krueger, kitty-corner to Kalila, propped at an angle, is fed through a gastronomy tube as well. His father never visits. Ghost-thin and awkward, the mother curls over her baby's emaciated body, fine hair masking her face. There's a nervousness in neonatal this afternoon. Like the restlessness of cows when one is led off to the slaughter. *Left on your own with your baby. It could happen.*

One last feeding lesson. 4 cc of Prosobee dribble down the elevated tube. I pour Prosobee from the narrow flask. Liquid gives in to gravity. The baby mews, moves softly in her bed. That little voice. 2 cc MCT oil spill down the tube. 1 cc digoxin.

Kalila stares up at me while the Prosobee drips. She senses something is afoot. Her legs kick once. Her orange Nerf ball springs across the isolette. I tighten the clip to slow the drops, pull up the stool, open the isolette hatch, and draw the little one onto my lap, tubes trailing like ribbons, like first prize at the fair. Kalila's small hand opens in a stationary wave. Goodbye, neonatal.

I hum, begin to sing. *Sail, baby, sail far across the sea.* Kalila gawks. Heads shoot up, the babies skittish. Kalila stares harder, a frown of concentration creasing her tiny forehead. You see? Just mention escape and this baby's on alert.

If you have any problems, the Dutch nurse says, stopping by Kalila's isolette, just call the hospital. She wrings my hand. You're very brave.

The social worker hovers, clipboard in hand. Marriages break up at times like this.

Screw off.

I'm here if you want to talk.

I turn my back. I am marching Kalila out of this hostile country, deserting its roads of tubes and intravenous lines, its trails of glass boxes, beeping machines, brown walls, closing doors, bequeathing them to the less determined, to those who don't know how to fight to win.

I replace the sleeping child in her glass cupboard, ride down the elevator, and step into a frigid blue-white world. Wind eddies the snow in swirling spirits. Storm in the forecast. In the time it takes to run across the giant parking lot to my car, my left cheek freezes. The Toyota's stiff motor barely turns. Five-thirty p.m. Dusk threads itself across the heavens.

One night to go.

I pull out of the hospital parking lot in a cloud of white exhaust, slide left onto Twenty-ninth Street, the terrible never-ending present vanishing in wisps of fog.

By the time I jerk up to the house, the interior of the car is almost warm.

Brodie

You hover at the living room window, ache in your joints, peer through an oval frame of frost, burst open the front door, run out without your jacket, carry in the toy-loaded baby seat, slip on the front steps, trip over Skipper's skittering paws, the porch so cold.

A world of sharp edges. You've cleaned and rearranged the house. So many places a child might come to harm. You've started supper, your cooking a nervous habit. The house smells of sweet and sour. Maggie drops her coat and boots. While you set the table, Maggie stands in the baby's room, peach-and-cream wallpaper. Orange is the most stimulating colour, the physiotherapist said.

While you ladle the food, Maggie wanders to the front window to look beyond to the duplex where your neighbour slouches in the window mornings, scratching his underwear. Where a little girl lives.

Tomorrow your own will live across the street.

Maggie

Sweet and sour pork ribs. Rice. Green beans. Baguette. Brodie spoons food into his mouth. Odd to be eating at a time like this. Sharing this Last Supper, remembering five months of grim and bloodless battle.

Brodie reaches for his glass, and as he raises his milk, the tears slide.

We'll do all right, Brodie.

I know.

I lie in bed and listen to the crunch of tires on the street, to Skipper's snuffly breaths. Imagine tomorrow's negations. No waiting for the phone. No long drive to the hospital. No walk into that cold neonatal country where dreams are unloaded at the door. A gaping space across from Baby Krueger's isolette. Will he sense Kalila's absence? Will he wonder where she's gone? Will the doctors, doing their rounds, experience a brief jerk of emotion? The chart for Kalila, thrown away? Her part played in hospital history over?

Last night, Marigold's girls burst through the door. A celebration. Last chance to babysit for a long time. Brodie popped their favourite disc into the DVD player, the two snuggled between us, Skipper scrunched at our feet, all chomping popcorn that still strews the carpet, and watched Mary Poppins and Eli dance their way through life's tribulations.

There are worlds beyond worlds and times beyond times ... and all of them, as children know, penetrate each other, Eli said. The girls drew against us, fresh-wind scent in their hair.

Outside, wind growls itself into a storm.

I twist to look at the alarm clock. Two a.m.

Four months, twenty-seven days.

Ten more hours.

Brodie

It is near noon when the white-and-yellow ambulance jerks onto the street piled high with snowdrifts.

Maggie!

Maggie at a run.

You watch at the window, skittering heart, the driver jumps down, kicks up a snow spray. You, out this morning, six a.m., scraping the sidewalk, head lifted to the west. White clouds scuttle a whiter sky. You've spent the morning hunched over physics lab reports, drinking coffee, scrawling with your red pen. The tall thin passenger flings open the back doors, lifts out a small glass box. They stumble through the drifts, a baby between them, airborne, gazing at white sky. Her container touches down. Snow-scraped cement.

Calgary, meet Kalila!

Kalila, Calgary!

Two strangers push a tiny child up the sidewalk, natural light enfolding itself round her for the first time, two awkward, swearing men, wheels catching in the snowdrifts, swoop this baby into air as they back up the stairs and stamp into the porch, fighting the awkward angles. Skipper crouched under the kitchen table, whining. The neighbour, face seamed, rumpled sweater, squinting across the street.

And it's happening. A tiny princess rolls through your living room, her coach trailing a track of dirty melting snow across the waiting carpet.

The moving men unload Kalila in her winter nursery. Two icemen, breathing out of sync, smelling of snow and cold and outdoor boots, unload a glass-box baby, oxygen tent zipping, tubes and hoses sorted, Kalila already tumbled into exhausted sleep, deep breathing on her back, hospital nightie abandoned, in a surprising little dress of lacy forest-green, a five-month-old newborn, arm flung above her head.

She sleeps just like her Grandma Watson! Maggie whispers.

The men tuck in the tent around her, turn the oxygen up to fifty-three per cent. For half an hour. Get her breathing.

Well.

This startling change.

Thank you.

Yes. Good luck.

Two shaking hands. Two shaking heads. A shutting door.

You stare down at a daughter. Skipper sticks his nose around the door. Your arms reach toward her crib and you engulf her, tubes and all, and not a soul to stop you. You gather all those bits of baby right into your arms.

Kalila.

She blows out mucus.

No.

It cannot be put off.

Practical Maggie reaching for the suction hose. You place shaking hands over the baby's cheeks.

Let's get it over with.

Kalila flails against blue-budded sheets. For those brief moments perhaps she thought her hell was over. Maggie shoving tubing down her nostril, green gunk sluffing up the tube. Snake out the hose and snake it in again. Kalila fighting, rasping, wheezing. Skipper begging to be let out the back door. You take over, stuff it in the other nostril, ears closed against the baby's cries. Kalila scrunched-faced, gasping. You unsnake the hose. Draw against you this bundle of exhausted baby.

Abusers that torture and then offer love.

A steady rush of cold oxygen into the baby's face.

Slowly the blueness clears.

Kalila light and startling rests within your arms. You look down into the little face and let go every preconception you ever held about the world. The child's here. Inside you opens a round flat disk, a cold grey stone of peace.

Kalila.

Autumn baby.

Little Kali.

Welcome home.

+

Outside the bedroom window, the thermometer reads minus twenty-nine.

It's warming.

You look at each other. Breathing history. Breathing cold.

You've weathered one more storm.

You will outstrip the odds.

February 28
History and Physical Examination
In spite of all Baby Solantz's problems, she
remains stable. At her parents' request, she
was discharged on February 27. Home per
transport isolette 47% oxygen. Gastrostomy
suspended on monitor. K. Slistan, *R.N.* attending
night nurse.

Brodie

You wake with a start. Lie still in darkness, letting your fears unclutch. They lift, unbuckle themselves, dissolve. Kalila!

You tear across the hall, nearly upending the night nurse, who gives a croaky shriek.

Good Lord! she says, hand to her jiggly breasts. Well, you're up now. I'll gather my things. The room alive with the sluff and sigh of equipment and machines. Kalila sleeps in a little ball of tangled blankets. The night nurse waves her goodbyes, heads out the door. One day. Day one. Maggie still asleep. The mobile circles like a universe of stars, patterning Kalila's blankets, sweeping shadow across her face. You steal close, unzip the oxygen tent.

> *Hush little baby, don't say a word*
> *Daddy's gonna buy you a mockingbird…*

Maggie appears, sleepy, hair stuck out, grinning ear to ear.

You spend the day cosied within Kalila's bedroom, blankets and pillows spread across the floor. An all-day picnic. Skipper lies half in, half out the bedroom door. You make Maggie a smiley face plate for lunch: bean-sprout-hair, broccoli-ears, cucumber-nose, a cherry-tomato-smile, orange dressing on the side. She breaks out laughing. Her old laugh, big and clean.

You take suctioning in tow. When Kalila dozes, you make love in the cradle of blankets and half-eaten plates. Fall asleep in a tangle of arms. That evening you order ginger beef, rent a video, lug the television into Kalila's room. Saturday Night at the Movies. You have agreed to *My Fair Lady!* Would agree to anything. You pop popcorn. Maggie mixes her favourite — ginger ale and orange juice.

Kalila. Her name a summer song between you.

Maggie drives you crazy singing along as characters burst into "The Rain In Spain," "I Could Have Danced All Night." You threaten to join in.

Kalila falls asleep in your arms during "On the Street Where You Live," but you won't put her in her crib. You circle her bead of belly button, that one scar lacing you all together. She sleeps, her blue-tipped fingers clinging to your hand. Maggie turns up the TV to hear over the chug and rumble of equipment.

At eleven you abandon Kalila to her blue-budded bed and

to the night nurse, popcorn trailing the floor from her room to yours. Fairy-tale crumbs to lead you back tomorrow.

You fall into your own bed, exhausted, imprinted with baby, and make love through old familiar paths.

Outside, the wind in song.

Maggie

Hell's bells! I'm a live whole mom, holding a live whole baby. There follow days of waking, grins plastered to our faces, sprinting to the adjoining bedroom. Kalila waiting, sweet and milky, or sour with morning bowels. Who cares? The baby's here, living the Happy Ever After.

Mom phones. Och, you must feel such heaviness on waking. I'm praying every day. This big responsibility.

Heaviness! I'm a free-flying cloud wisping an azure sky. Life's joyous mystery maps our days.

We shall not all sleep. But we shall all be changed, in a moment, in the twinkling of an eye.

Electricity flows, lightning-wild, from my fingers, down my arms, to a baby girl who startles at my touch.

Brodie!

Three days in a row Kalila wakes up smiling. I hold her whenever I want, lie down with her however I want, support her tiny back whatever time I want, and help her do her situps.

Mom things. The sun shines through winter glass. We become downright adept at suctioning. A partnership. It doesn't take that long.

Brodie

You make dinner while Maggie shops and pays the bills.
While she clears the dishes, and tidies up the kitchen, you
slip into the child's bedroom, draw Kalila on your lap, she
stares upside down into your face. At the sound of your voice,
she grabs your finger and goes absolutely still.

> *The fox said, For me you're only a little boy just like*
> *a hundred thousand other little boys. And I have*
> *no need of you. And you have no need of me, either.*
> *For you I'm only a fox like a hundred thousand*
> *other foxes. But if you tame me, we'll need each*
> *other. You'll be the only boy in the world for me.*
> *I'll be the only fox in the world for you.*
>
> *I'm beginning to understand, the little prince*
> *said. There's a flower...I think she's tamed me.*
>
> *Possibly, said the fox. On Earth, one sees all*
> *kinds of things.*

You move a little worktable into Kalila's room. Spread out your books. Mark labs. Make notes:

Entanglement: the most perplexing phenomenon in the world of quantum mechanics. Two particles may be very far apart, thousands of kilometres. But whatever happens to one of them causes immediate change in the other. You lay aside your notes, and Skipper rises stiffly. You pick Kalila up and, cords stretching, walk her to the window. You stand, all three, looking into the dark awake with moon. Daddy. Daughter. Dog.

Your long strand of lonely life threads into three. You begin to talk, it's true that you talk physics, but still you talk.

Did you know that the first real breakthrough in measuring the distances of the solar system didn't come till 1761?

Did you know that the naked eye can see six thousand stars?

Did you know that it was thanks to a blackout in Los Angeles during the Second World War that allowed the American astrologer Walter Baade to make a detailed study of the Andromeda galaxy? Imagine. A war revealed the stars.

The days skim by. Each day the sky stays lighter longer.

Marigold and her girls come over for twice-weekly visits. No tourist visas necessary. They're free to come and go. Francine and Suzette take turns holding Kalila while the other holds the hose. They trace her tiny shoulders, transfixed, gentle, mystified.

Maggie and Marigold chat about Marigold's French course, about the unusually cold winter. Marigold's eyes fill up with tears. She says that Kalila looks lovely, absolutely lovely. The girls kiss and kiss and kiss their little cousin. You snap pictures, zipping about like a carefree boy.

After nine days the community nurse rings the doorbell. Kalila's growing, she announces, after transferring the baby to her portable scale. She weighs eleven ounces more. Her head is getting bigger. And she's more alert. Of course. She's with her mommy and daddy now. She's home, this little growing daughter.

The woman jots her notes and breezes out, leaving the carefree aura of approaching summer.

Maggie

The eleventh day we hold an impromptu baby shower. Marigold's idea. No one has seen Kalila. It's time she meets the world. Marigold bustles in for the day, and we bake a dozen varieties of little cakes and cookies. The house smells like a holiday. The goodies sit on the dining-room table, looking festive and elegant, offsetting the white lace table-cloth.

Brodie sets up in the bedroom, Kalila perched on his lap, oxygen hose to her face, suctioning when necessary. Skipper plants himself at Brodie's feet, facing them on point. Francine and Suzette squish tight on either side. Kalila tilts, neck supported, a little button of a thing in her frilly white dress and booties. A constellation. No glass obscures her now.

The doorbell chimes and chimes and chimes. The girls race ahead, shrieking.

Come see Kalila! Come see our baby cousin! Now!

The little house crowds to overflowing. Skipper, paws crunched by one-too-many high-heeled shoes, skulks to the basement, while the women exclaim over chocolate cheesecake brownies, carrot cake with cream cheese icing, poppyseed cupcakes, platters of exotic fruits and cheeses, greeting one another with anxious cries of recognition, settling on chairs and sofa, ignoring the girls.

Come *on!* Francine and Suzette grab hands, drag unwilling feet toward the bedroom door. The women apprehensive, clustering in twos and threes.

How abnormal will she be? their nervous smiles ask. Deformed? What do we say? No. You go first. No really. After you.

Brodie, grinning.

But she's lovely, the women sing. Look at your pretty cousin!

She's almost a normal baby! Suzette says proudly. We treat her just the same!

I feel beautiful. A yummy mummy. I don't give a shit what these designer women think. Girls! Fetch the gifts!

Everyone crowds into the living room to watch the girls rip open one fancy-papered, daintily-ribboned package after another. Marigold takes turns handing each a gift and records the giver while Suzette and Francine volleyball the discarded paper.

Colourful clowns.

Storybooks for two- to five-year-olds.

Outfits up to 6X.

A little backpack.

Gifts for Kalila's future.

I lie awake long after the guests have gone and the paper is bagged, leftover dainties returned to the fridge, the creak of the kitchen floor, the night nurse sampling a plateful. Brodie's steady breaths beside me. I lie in darkness, eyes fixed on the stars.

Maggie

I've been a real mom sixteen days when Kalila's gastrostomy tube drops out. The baby is sleeping while I have a go at making bread. First time I've tried her in the cradle Larry made before her birth. I'm kneading the dough when a thump hails Kalila's hoarse and whispered cries. I drop the wooden spoon and run. The baby's weight has rocked the cradle, she's slid against the side, ready to drop onto the floor. The tube has shot right out of her stomach in a mess of porridge-looking goo.

Oh, Jesus.

I stand, neck cranked, hands sticky with bread dough. Our baby has a hole, a hole crusted with scabby pus. It smells. A rotten stink. Kalila purrs. Skipper is licking it. I shove the dog, right the baby in the cradle, trip over Skipper, knock him out of the way, decorating him with bread dough and drops of flour, try to stuff the rubber tube back in; the hose won't go. The baby cries sharp bird cries.

Shit! I dial the hospital's telephone number with shaking fingers. The porridge moves out, in, out from the baby's gut like something alive.

Lord Jesus. Fifth floor, please. Neonatal.

An endless pause.

Neonatal. Carol Hunt, head nurse.

It's fallen out the tube into her stomach Kalila — Maggie — Watson Solantz my baby's gastrostomy her stomach's pouring out it won't go back she's still she isn't moving her insides are gushing —

A rustling. Muted voices.

The voice comes back on the line. Mrs. Solantz. Our records say that you've withdrawn this child from our hospital.

God! Of course. I know! I've, yes, we took — she's falling apart here . . .

A crackling line. — suggest you phone your family doctor, Mrs. Solantz.

No! This is the baby you — she *lived* there, for God's sake! Is there someone in charge?

Mrs. Solantz. Such a reasonable voice. *I'm* in charge. You've withdrawn your child from our care. Hospital policy. Our records say your baby's been discharged.

⁜

The startled taxi driver ushers me tangled up in tubes, out the door, taxi driver, baby, me, an awkward three-step, stumbling, slipping on the stairs, oxygen tank, blotting tissues, oxygen hose, the sliding porridge goo. Skipper whining behind the slammed door.

The mountains razor-sharp against Calgary's skyline. This city rife with red lights, pedestrian crosswalks, school zones. *Bloody hell!* I park my eyes on the taxi driver's chewed-down fingernails.

Two adults and a baby sidestep in the clinic door.

Brodie takes exactly twenty-three minutes, leaving delighted grade elevens with a last-period spare.

Our family doctor reinserts the tube, regards our faces. You're brave, he says. He says this very gently. You shouldn't have tried to stick the tube back in. Leave doctors' work to doctors. Here, it's not life-threatening. Gastrostomy tubes slip out. Sliding relief of tears. All three of us head back into cheery winter sunshine. Kalila yawning, fisting out her eyes.

We've had an outing.

There. You see? To hell with the bloody hospital. We'll do fine on our own.

Maggie

We step through calendar pages. Day eighteen, day nineteen, day twenty-three. An Upjohn worker phones, sets up a house call. How's that baby doing? A routine checkup. Dustballs crowd behind the sofa. I clean. Scrub the spotted kitchen floor. Put an incensed Skipper outside. Measure out digoxin. Water my thirsty plants, which throw back their tendrils and suck the water in. They know they must look good. I clear out the suction tube. Kalila coos. Scrub the brown scum from the kitchen sink, pop in to shout Hi! to Kalila, unhook the tubes, change a diaper, rehook, rinse a jam jar, check on the baby, wash and iron the curtains. Rehang them. Bake the scones.

She's coming to see that Kalila's okay, she's not going to write a housekeeping report, Brodie jokes as he heads off to work.

I dust the picture frames, clean out the hall closet, make coffee, scrub down the kitchen cupboards. Am wiping baseboards when the doorbell rings.

Jasmine Forester says, I'm here from Foothills —

I stare at her name tag. From Upjohn?

No, from Foothills Hospital.

Well. This is unexpected.

I usher the woman in. She has brought the smell of wind-tossed clothes. A whiff of ice.

She's here to check that the heart monitor is working.

Ah. A lady of the heart. It's working fine. I'm actually expecting —

Jasmine Forester steps past me into my spotless house.

The doorbell. Jasmine Forester gets there first, lets in a stranger.

A pleasure to meet you, the two say to each other. Jasmine Forester. Noreen Marks.

I'm Maggie, I announce. But it's like grade three on the playground. They've already made friends. I speed to get the coffee. Set out white-chocolate-and-blueberry scones and cream and jam. Have I cleaned enough? What if they want decaf? Do I look like a mother? I retie my apron sash and lead the Upjohn woman into Kalila's room. The heart monitor woman follows. Kalila peers up at us.

Three women peer down. Pride rushes my veins. What this child has survived. What she — just look at her!

Could I speak with you in the living room? the Upjohn woman says.

Sure, I say. Sure, the heart monitor lady says.

Well. This is unexpected.

The two of them pull the bedroom door shut on their way out. I stand in the centre of Kalila's rumbling bedroom, which smells of Prosobee and medication. Look at the heart monitor machine, which Jasmine Forester neglected to check. Look at my baby, who stares back at me, look out the window to a white March landscape, look at my watch. Gravity slowly giving up its hold. Goosebumps ride my skin. I want my sweater, which is lying over a dining room chair, making my house look messy.

Kalila throws her head from side to side, turns blue, blows mucus. Oh, for crying out loud! Kalila! No! Not! Now! Quit! It! Please! I snatch the tube, down, down the baby's nose. I've learned in Brodie's absence how to clasp the baby's head in the crook of my elbow, which frees my left hand. I suction, suction, steel-backed against Kalila's cries. Small cheeks within my hands, the baby quiets, gums her lips, looks grievously at me.

The moment I step out into the hall of our tiny house, I am upon the women, who are standing, heads bowed together, as if in prayer. The Upjohn woman brushes her hands against her skirt like she's been baking. Cooking up an idea, it turns out. Mrs. Solantz! she says, as if I'd yelled boo. The women take a sudden breath; eyes meet. They look away.

Mrs. Solantz, the Upjohn contract is to be reviewed, and renewed — if necessary — every second week. Ms. Marks waves an airy hand. I'm sure you've read it. You are doing a fine job here, you and your husband. She looks around my newly mopped and vacuumed house.

Jasmine Forester claps her hands. Did you just suction the baby?

Yes, I did. I look at the impeccable Jasmine Forester, whose lime suit is highlighted by her sunshine-yellow-and-lime scarf.

My, but you're efficient.

Isn't she doing well!

Jasmine Forester has placed an interested expression over her professional one, as if she is hearing the Upjohn woman's words for the first time.

So very well, in what, I'm sure, are difficult circumstances. Does your husband help?

Of course, I say icily.

Yes? the women beam and nod. Everyone is smiling.

As you know, Mrs. Solantz, the Upjohn woman slips her shoe off and on her foot in a kind of foolish shuffle, we were just discussing, this service costs the taxpayer a lot. I'll be frank. An awful lot.

There are needy children, the heart monitor woman says compassionately, in this very city.

I'll be in touch, says Noreen Marks while Jasmine Forester faces pleasantly forward, intent, as if listening to a speech. I'll be in touch with the doctors at the Foothills — she clears her throat. But, she coughs here, really, you're doing well, so very well, that at the end of the next two-week period, I will recommend that Upjohn services are no longer needed. In your case.

Light fogs. What do you mean?

Why, you're so very competent. You'll do fine on your own.

But — how will I do the shopping?

Your husband? the heart monitor lady suggests.

But we don't — who'll pay for the equipment?

After some time Noreen Marks says, I believe —

There is a lie in believe.

— there are other people, less efficient. Frankly, they need it more.

Jasmine Forester, who has nothing to do with Upjohn, nothing at all, excuses herself and checks the heart monitor, which, she declares gleefully, is working. The Upjohn woman, with whom she has struck up a bosom buddy friendship in my tidy living room, hangs about the house until Ms. Forester's work is finished, and they head out together.

A lovely little house, the heart monitor lady says, as they step into the porch, down my lovely little stairs, and into cold March sunshine.

+

The house is golden with late-afternoon light when I make my way back to Kalila's room. I pass my untouched scones. The drying homemade jam. The cradle, abandoned in a dusty sunbeam, Kalila sucking on her tongue. Tsk tsk tsk. Her palms are flat open, one lying upon the other, as if interrupted in a hand game. Her eyes follow me. She has a tiny double chin. I look at the bones in Kalila's hands, hands stained brown and blue from intravenous lines. *Twenty-three days. Twenty-three days I've had with you. Just fourteen more.*

A discordant scale slides backward, forward, backward. My breaths come through a gaping hole. How will we suction the baby without the machine? How will we know if, during the night, Kalila slips into a bradycardia, suffers cardiac arrest? Kalila stares at me, one hand curls into a fist. The fist slides to her mouth. Tsk. Tsk. I'm slapped with sudden knowledge. The baby's hungry. I'm thirty-four minutes late with feeding. What kind of mother doesn't feed her child? An unmother. That's who. My hands shake as I secure the tube, pinch the tag that slows the feeding to a slow drip, pour 4 cc of Prosobee into the test tube attached to Kalila's stomach tube.

Kalila, I cleaned the house for you.

I cleaned too well.

I grope for the child who expels a little breath of air. Haaa.

We work out a system after Brodie phones Upjohn for the seventh time. We'll lose the night nurse but keep the equipment. I stop walking Skipper altogether. I clean tubes, scrub floors, bake bread, tell Kalila stories. Damn every-fuckingbody. We will not give in.

Brodie

BEEE-BEEEE-BEEE. You are on your feet and running before either of you is awake. A red light blinks in the semi-darkness where Kalila thrashes. 96-94-92 reads the heart monitor printout. Turn her over! Shake her! Brodie! Flex her arms! 84-82-80. For God's sake! 77-74. Press on her ribcage!

You stand in grey predawn. The clock reads 4:04 a.m.

Kalila, colour restored, breathes the quick breaths of a baby.

You replace the oxygen tent around her crib, ensuring the plastic is tucked within the bumper.

In bed, not touching, you listen to the dawn: dog bark, birdsong, repeated squeal of tires in the street.

Maggie

For three days the baby gags, coughs phlegm, croons thickly in her throat.

It's because her lungs are congested, the cardiologist says over the phone. Bring her in at month's end.

Domestic rituals abandoned, I turn to the Yellow Pages. Phone a new cardiologist. Beg an appointment. Turn on the radio. The days are getting longer, the announcer says. I cannot take longer days.

Brodie takes the afternoon off school. The new cardiologist, Dr. Rosewood, thin, blue sweater, no static cling, no doctor's coat, examines Kalila with long fine fingers, examines her as if the only thing in the world is this small dusky baby. At her touch, Kalila stills. After some time, the doctor sets her stethoscope aside, regards us, stuck together like glue.

What is a baby this blue doing out of the hospital?

We stare at the floor, two misbehaving school kids, caught in the act.

This babe needs heart surgery. Dr. Rosewood sits down on her stool. She contemplates us. Now.

There is an ordinariness about Dr. Rosewood. Her face is frank, not moral, not sealed up. Look at her. A doctor who sees possibility, who dares to see the whole.

I fall in love with Dr. Rosewood then and there. It is a fierce and angry love: in love with her skinniness, her saggy sweater, her pale and freckled face. Her sharp insistence.

Brodie looks like he's caught hold of something he didn't know he'd lost.

In this way, it is settled. No fanfare. We relinquish Kalila back into the glare of lights, this time to the Children's Hospital. March 30. The child is five months, twenty-four days old.

No worries, the doctor says. She's not a newborn. Go home. Get some rest.

Brodie

The glass house cradled the princess as an oyster cradles a pearl. Then one day her glass walls shifted, and the princess knew the caress of wind, the wheeling touch of sun, the melody of rain.

This little princess tasted hope, salty on her tongue.

Maggie

Day four. Go home and pack a suitcase. The nurses' strike is on. Only one hospital in the province performing heart surgery.

Everything happens at once. Snatching up scattered clothes, the goodbye kisses, suppressed excitement, the taxi ride to the airport. Kalila loaded on the little plane.

Bucking headwinds, the draughty airplane arrows north. Sun in my eyes, squashed against a frozen window, I stare down at patchwork quilts of white, mouse-brown, glacier-blue, snagged through by frozen tinsel. Kalila's isolette takes up most of the space behind the pilot. The hospital staff hovers, backs to me. We speed through the sky toward icy Edmonton.

An ambulance screams onto the runway as we bump down, doors flung ajar, the baby, then I, deposited inside. Doors barely closed, it skids off in a flash of lights and wailing sirens.

Cut the melodrama! What's the fuss? It's no big deal. A routine operation. I don't want my baby a star. I just want life to reconvene. But the ambulance driver is a lunatic, careening corners, whizzing red lights. Watch me! Watch me! And thanks to Mr. Friggin' Action, the people of Edmonton do. They stand on street corners and stare at two lives streaking past. Kalila wheezewheezewheezing on the ride.

An orderly waits as the ambulance screeches to a halt. He wheels her through the doors. The baby disappears. I leap out in pursuit, suitcase banging my legs. The wards are in disarray. Patients mixed up in every unit. Beds stuck in any bit of space. The hospital staff ignores me. Sorry, god knows where a baby might have gone.

I locate her finally on the seventh floor in a wing of seven patients. With the exception of Kalila, all are adult. The doughy man beside Kalila's isolette tried to kill himself last night. Nurses run bleating in all directions, annoyed at inconsiderate Donald, whose six-foot-four frame hangs off the bed like his knee joints and elbows belong to someone else.

Come on, Donald.

Turn over, Donald.

You're a big man, Donald, feed yourself.

Sit up, Donald.

Donald, for Pete's sake, lift your arms.

Donald's placid body doesn't want to cooperate. The nurses prod him, shove him, roll him over, roll their eyes, force down his medication. Donald squeezes his eyes tight against the stares.

I plunk my suitcase down beside Kalila's isolette. It and the end of Donald's bed are lightly touching. I discreetly push her the last few centimetres toward the wall. Is this grab for death catching? I eye Donald's muddled sheets. *Park at your own risk.*

I locate a washroom, throw up. The frigging ambulance driver's fault. When I return, the nurse says, Oopsie-daisy! Honey, please wait in the hall.

What for?

Your baby. We have to suction her. This nurse with a rubber band around her ponytail lowers her voice clandestinely. It's not pretty to watch.

The prim young woman disappears into the chaos. I stand in the hall until the light turns grey. I haven't been punished so since elementary school. Home lies like a book abandoned, three hundred kilometres away. Brodie on a kitchen chair in the dim light, grading physics papers, back bent in a hopeful question mark.

✢

On the third morning I walk into that hospital room, Kalila isn't there. An empty hole looms where her isolette sat. Donald squints against the world. A kind nurse deposits me in a chair. She's gone for tests is all, Mrs. Solantz, there now — laughing — Honey, she's only gone for tests.

All sadness flaps out the window as if it had a pair of

207

wings. I am left strangely rattled, but in a lovely sort of way. Donald opens his eyes, nose whistling, and stares at the empty spot.

You can try to die in here.

Donald's eyes shift vacantly toward my voice.

But you're not going to. This is a hospital. And it's equipped to save.

⁺

It's past noon when Kalila returns, asleep on the ride. An hour passes. Wind wheels against the building. I sit by the window. Snow devils. A scarlet running shoe tossed against the snow. An overturned shopping cart. Lines of streaking cars. An agitated orderly is elbowing me aside. The tests are good.

What?

They're going to operate.

The baby already hurtling out of sight.

Go back to the hotel. We'll call you when it's over. You have the best heart surgeon in Western Canada. Get yourself something to eat.

Two little sausages frying in a pan, Donald says to the empty square of floor. One went pop, the other went BAM!

⁺

Cold slices my neck. Minus twenty-eight degrees and dropping. I leap from the taxi, race through the hotel's reception area, sprays of snow clumps draining on the carpet.

I jab the elevator button. Take the stairs two at a time, hurl myself into the room.

Brodie! They're doing it! Now! They're fixing her now! She's in! I am laughing, crying, falling off a cliff, the pages of the book no longer stuck. Our lives at last are lurching out of stall.

I flop against the headboard. Whew. Pick up the Gideon Bible from the dresser's top drawer. Hold in my hands my mother's faith. I crack it open. I Kings.

> Then came there two women that were harlots unto
> the king and stood before him. And the one woman
> said, I and this woman dwell in one house, and
> I was delivered of a child with her in the house.
> And it came to pass the third day after that I was
> delivered, that this woman was delivered also...
> And this woman's child died in the night because
> she overlaid it. And she arose at midnight and took
> my son from beside me, while thine handmaid slept,
> and laid it in her bosom, and laid her dead child in
> my bosom. And when I rose in the morning to give
> my child suck, behold, it was dead; but when I had
> considered it in the morning, behold, it was not my
> son which I did bear. And the other woman said,
> Nay, the living is my son, and the dead is thy son.
> Thus they spake before the king... And the king

said, Bring me a sword. And they brought a sword
before the king. And the king said, Divide the living
child in two, and give half to the one, and half to the
other. Then spake the woman whose the living child
was unto the king, for her bowels yearned upon her
son, and she said, O Lord, give her the living child,
and in no wise slay it. But the other said, Let it be
neither mine nor thine, but divide it. Then the King
answered and said, Give the first the living child,
and in no wise slay it, for she is the mother thereof.

Unmother. Mother.

I have kept my child whole.

I lift the receiver. Picture my mother, in the quiet of her bedroom, feeling for the phone.

That quiet calm. Hello?

Mom? She's in the operation. Mom. The baby's finally strong.

And my mother, awakened to her darkened world, feels her bedroom flood with prism colour, birdsong.

Maggie. Och yea. You don't know how I've prayed.

Ask anything in My name.

Desire spurts like anger. You have to want enough.

I slide the space between the hours. The slipping lights of cars. My body aches as if I'd run for miles. Love happens to you. There's nothing you can do. You fall headlong, chaotic, buckling. Your childhood dislodged, life a lost and found. Film looping years, moments, a tumbling slide show.

The phone rings, three sounding notes.

Hello?

Mrs. Solantz.

Watson. Laughing — Yes, it's — Mrs. Solantz. The words sail toward me. The operation's over.

Oh. Thank God.

Your baby's attached to a support system.

Sure.

…blood circulating through a machine — heart patched —

Yup.

— isn't breathing on her own — surgeon's concern — blood tainted —

There is light. There are voices. Someone says words. More words.

Words say themselves:

We can't hold her. She's gone.

A sound like water
Wind in the eaves
Snow shower sliding from a spruce
An open bracelet
She merges with the storm.

Hell of a night, the taxi driver says.

University Hospital, please. My chest corroded calcium, scraped inside of a kettle.

Somewhere a telephone wire hums, one beautiful clear tone.

You sick? Yea, goddamn nurses strike. Hell of a night to — Good luck! the driver shouts against my closing door.

✢

Mrs. Solantz.

The surgeon walks the light-filled corridor to meet me.

I try to make this moment last.

I try to hold the future out.

The future hurtles toward me.

— fixed her heart. It was the lungs —

Notes rests sharps flats.

Tenuto.

Kick of wind.

A body chopped by air.

We stand in an empty corridor.

His eyes are hazel.

I see he hasn't slept in days.

He jolts awake. Reaches for the phone.

The dog makes three small yips from its closed mouth.

He breathes the silence.

They stand, a man, a woman, connected by a wire, trying to contain this knowledge, trying to keep it small.

Light waves stab, deflect around him. The world rockets away. The night is a tight hem. Outside, the wind, the hills, the dirt, the rocks, the trees. The ice.

The galaxy.

A needlework of stars.

She rises
scattering, plunging mist
absence, presence

Ne me quitte pas.

April 2: Patient pronounced dead at 19:48.

The flick of a light switch.
Gone.

11:02 p.m. She enters the frozen plane. Enters a frozen plain.

Harsh light inside the cockpit.

Glazed windows. Airport lights. Cold stars. No moon.

The sun shall not smite thee by day nor the moon by night.

A life of Braille.

She places this life on top of her life. And now begins forever.

And a voice was heard in Ramah, lamentation and bitter weeping. Rachael weeping for her children, and would not be comforted.

He changed her diaper.
He told her a story.
He sang her a lullaby.

A child made it halfway round the sun.

There was a baby.
She died.

The sisters arrange a phone fan-out.
She's gone. The baby's gone.
One organizes flowers: wisteria, lily of the valley, sunflower, bird of paradise. Another chooses Scripture readings. *I will lift up mine eyes unto the hills from whence cometh my help — And Jesus said, Suffer the little children to come unto me.*

Hymn books scatter at yet another's feet.
"As a Mother Comforts Her Child"; "Under His Wings"; "My God and I."

The oldest will fly home from Australia.

They will do special singing. It's been how many years since they've sung together, but they will do this for her.

The man and woman push themselves into the gaudy pink funeral home on Centre Street. No. Cremate her. Fist searing the woman's chest. She wants the baby warm.

Strange sobbing women arrive on her doorstep, letting in streams of pale and frigid light, the dog in a skidding bark each time the doorbell rings. Women laden with cinnamon buns, tuna noodle casseroles, three-bean salads, fresh-baked dinner rolls. The woman leaves these gifts to dry out on the counter. Her sisters bake them, heat them, freeze them, bustle, eat them, put meals on the table.

The April wind sings.

Go outside. It will do you good. Her sisters send her out into the sunny gusts, into the chill of the day, like they used to do when she was little. She walks the Bow River, sightless, slashed by wind. Thinks of Moses bringing down the Ten Commandments. Naming them. Breaking them. Abandoned in the wilderness, wandering for forty years.

The man sits alone in the darkened bedroom and thinks transforming lead to gold.

The woman dresses in her dark green pinstriped suit. Steps into wind and sunlight. The man at the back step, still polishing his shoes. Far out on the horizon, the sky harbours green. They drive, chinook wind chanting, enter the church to Zamfir's flute. The sisters, a circling throng.

One yellow rose blooms on the altar.

An old teacher the woman hasn't seen in years waits in the foyer. Pain-tightened lips, his light rosewater smell. Small feet. Grey beard rough against her cheek.

They walk the aisle, a gauntlet of reaching hands, take their place in the front pew.

The sisters rise to sing.

No. Wait. No. Don't. It's happening so fast. The sisters step in line.

Faith is an acorn grown into an oak
Faith is Autumn in her burnished cloak

They turn their grief-filled faces, one, features dissolving, the others, stiff and grim, launch into high tenor, soprano, alto, middle-aged women looking foolish, incomplete, the oldest galloping the piano keys. The Watson girls perform.

Faith is the blackbird that sings before the dawn...

Our faith is shaken. A reed shattered in the wind. The minister's hand lights on the yellow rose. In the midst of our pain, what is there to sustain us? She moves around the pulpit. Outside melody of wind and landscape. We whistle in the dark when we're afraid. An African woman sings through the pain of childbirth. And the Russians. The Russians have always had a fantastic ear for music.

The man hears her voice through waves of water, bending light.

The Russian army in the First World War had a special position for a chosen soldier: not the lookout, not the bugler, no, the most honoured position was for the one who starts the song. When those Russian soldiers couldn't sing, when suffering choked their voices, they gleaned strength from the one whose job it was to start the song. The minister sets aside her notes. Looks at the couple. Today you cannot sing;

the will is gone. But your sisters start the song for you. One day grace will blow through you like the holy spirit's wind, and something of music will be born in you again. Outside wind rushes the grasses, whistling through hollow reeds.

A cousin rises, flute in hand. Music keens, sharp-strung debris:

A shame she couldn't die at birth.

This will make you a better person.

I'm holding off on buying a gift until, you know, we're sure.

Well, the Lord giveth and the Lord taketh away.

Remember, if this one doesn't — you can always have another.

You're getting time to recover without two a.m. feedings!

Be careful. Don't get too attached.

It's not your fault.

I'm sorry. She's been discharged.

The dappled flute notes transport them to the sunlit foyer.

The man reaches, wrists aching, holding up the world.

It's hard to understand.

A time of sorrow leads the way to a stronger faith.

The dark today can sometimes lead to light tomorrow.

Mr. Solantz. We're awfully sorry, sir.

You cannot predict where an electron will be in the next second. But when it's measured, its world splits into multiple universes.

May God comfort you in your loss.

Och, there's so little we can say.

The man reaching in the receiving line holds tight to hands, tries not to disappear.

The church empties. The man and the woman stand pressed together in the windswept churchyard. Are herded downstairs to the funeral luncheon. They fulfill their griefly obligations until the dusk of late afternoon writes itself against the sky, then they move toward the car, the sisters clucking round them, tucking in the woman's scarf, clinging to the man's hand, this walk, this long day ending.

Will you be all right? We froze the food. Don't cook. We'll call. Fingers laced. Tremulous smiles.

They drive away on singing tires to step across their crooked sidewalk. The walk they crossed, joyous, to birth a child six endless months ago. A dog steps out the open door to greet them. This place of stone the night the child came.

Snow is melting on the sidewalk steps. The sky in chaos, birds in swooping song. A ginger butterfly explodes in flight between the poplar branches.

The man thinks, So many quantum leaps.

The pain is like the light. Its waves go on and on.

I opened to my beloved, but my beloved was gone. I sought her, but I could not find her. I called her, but she gave me no answer.

The woman steps out into afternoon April sunlight. The neighbour across the street is mowing the lawn while her husband drowses on the porch steps. Spring's flightiness. The husband jolts awake. His gaze follows the woman pushing the lawn mower against the sunlight. Everywhere puddles shine. First week of springlike weather, enough to melt the snow. Vestiges of winter, gone. Life no longer safely frozen.

The street is deserted. Another hour and denim-clad teenagers will stream onto Charleswood Drive, shoving one another, high-stepping through puddles, in love with the crazy sun, with the crazy thrust of summer.

The screen door closes. The man makes his way down the steps. In the woman's hands, a small vase shielded in a mulberry cloth bag. Two cats appear, parade the sidewalk. Tails high, they meander down Charlebois, the drone of the lawn mower reassuring on the pitching breeze.

The woman stops at the sidewalk. The neighbour grins at her. The glare of sunshine shivers new green buds. The woman brushes hair out of her eyes. The slouched husband waves back.

The man and woman step onto the road, wait for a car to cross, then start in silence up the street. Piano notes dapple the air. Such intense sunlight. Light cuts through everything.

The soft growl of a dog. Abandoned chairs against a patio. The woman's heart is strained. She is so tired now. The road is empty, the only moving objects this April afternoon, a man, a woman, one neighbour, two cats skulking through the hedge, spring buds.

They cross Capri, head north and west, the line of houses breaks away and becomes parkland, the earth's heat rises; overhead, rocking blue sky. They pass a park, mount the street, Nose Hill brown hay above them. When they reach John Laurie Boulevard, the man takes the bag, her hand, as they wait in the churn of cars, straight-backed against the wind, the honk of horns, the dust.

A space opens in traffic, and they run, stop on the boulevard, shirts twirling, they blow across, buried in windy clothes.

And now they start the long climb up Nose Hill.

I am the rose of Sharon and the lily of the valley. As a lily among thorns is my love amongst the daughters.

There is a lovely winding path that leads off the paved thoroughfare onto Nose Hill. You can catch it at the Brisbois turnoff. Just beyond a twist of bush and briar, the path breaks into three. It heads west toward Shaganappi, straight up, or east toward the Winter Club. The east path winds upward behind a half-kilometre row of poplars, hides the climber behind a rise of hill so there is country on all sides.

The man and woman take the east path, dissolve into greenery. Restless wind, ripping landscape, wild grasses, breezy sunlight. They move, two figures, over a burned-out patch of hill until they reach the summit. Wild roses thorn ravines. Their fragrance on the wind. The shimmer of quivering reeds. One crocus under snow.

I am my beloved's; her desire is toward me.

Light falls. It bends and scales, colours collide, as swirled by sunlit gusts, she lifts her hands.

Releases to the wind.

On a wind and light-filled Monday morning Jasmine Forester, the lady of the heart, presents herself at the door in a pale lavender suit with matching scarf and earrings. Here, she informs the woman, to retrieve the heart monitor.

The lady of the heart steps into the baby's bedroom. Machines still chug. No one has entered this room. No one has shut down life support. The constant curve of time.

The door sighs open.

She pulls the plug.

Absolute zero.

Outside, a swallow sings.

I'm sorry your daughter is dead, Jasmine Forester says from the safety of the doorstep. Her words scatter down the stairs in tumbling particles of light. How was anyone to know the child was so ill?

The clicks of her high-heeled shoes tapdance the afternoon away.

The woman climbs Nose Hill. Voices. A chorus. Listen. Listen. Who knows what this earth holds. How many ashes have caught the wind as loved ones swallowed light and let them go.

The sage and silence of this place.

It's springtime. The first rains wash old dust. The earth in song.

Where does a child end, where does the earth begin?

The man drives to school through stars and sunsets, through the twist and turn of seasons. Enters his small, new-smelling apartment, leaving lights off as he goes.

Home alone nights in this strange space he feels the habit of the woman's hands. An arch of foot. Hollow of underarm. Hears her voice saying crazy, indignant words, he hears her laughing stories; her voice stays with him evenings as if she's at the kitchen door.

She might have been a forest ranger, she said those first days after.

Putting away the milk, She'd have liked archeology. Scratching scar into possibility until he could have choked. And when he wouldn't answer: Say it. Say her name.

With time, people slip into their names. The child's left open. No time to enter it. No time to be it. How could he explain his need to have the silence cradle her.

How could he explain what's buried must stay buried.

How could he explain there's no such thing as time.

He read and reads.

If someone loves a flower, of which just one single blossom grows in all the millions and millions of stars... The important thing is what can't be

seen... If you love a flower that lives on a star,
then it's good at night, to look up at the sky. And all
the stars are blossoming... He can say to himself,
"Somewhere, my flower is there..."

The man's son doesn't ask about a baby born in this western city, in another life. And the man doesn't speak of her. The boy visits in the summers. He is almost seven now. The man drives the boy to baseball games, to ice cream shops; they fly a kite; they walk along the river and the man explains light waves.

He keeps the baby separate, hinged in windy landscape. Skin starred by moonlight. Scars criss-crossing her heels.

Dust, seasons, scars and weather, pages turn, the city grows. The woman's sisters send her to Banff for a massage. Take a day away. Go for a drive. Her thirty-seventh birthday. Her husband gone eight years. Summer ending. The woman drives toward granite mountains, toward a late August afternoon. The car speeds into sunlight, into wind, then rain. The sun comes out again, illuminates wet pavement. The woman slides toward mountains on the lull of summer tires.

Banff is busy with seduced tourists, grabbing elusive summer heat. The woman winds her way past in her small Toyota, over the bridge to a distant part of town. A wrinkled Hungarian woman opens the door to a private dwelling. The woman steps inside.

A high cot waits in the tiny living room. The woman disrobes, climbs naked onto the narrow table, skin cool, then wanting, beneath a yellowed sheet.

The old one has efficient hands. Forceful, they stroke the woman's wrists, forearms, her feet, move into curve and swell, their rhythm steady, strong. The woman closes her eyes.

Who's Rose?

The woman jolts on her narrow bed. Why — Rose? — well, she's my sister.

The old one works the woman's temples, jaw bone, rhymes her hands across the woman's freckled shoulders. She has a zippy personality, your sister?

Rose? The woman struggles to sit up; the old one's firm hands hold her down.

Tell her not to drive through any yellow lights.

The woman's language scatters like wingtips of startled birds. A strong pull down and down and down — buttocks, thighs, circling behind her knees, her calves, her skin tingling the length of its desire.

The room fills with the scent of buttercup and wild rose. The woman on her back. Like a mother kneading bread dough, the Hungarian works the woman's bones. A stillness from some other place. Lost words. Light passing on the ceiling. The old one's hands. Nearby the river flows. A droning bee travels the window. Cars shift out on the road. Fused light the colour of summer grain.

Who's this? The old hands arrest on the woman's breast-bone. A child. She's dead. She's here.

I adjure you, O daughters of Jerusalem, if you find my beloved that you tell her I am sick with love.

I didn't know you would come back.

The child's hair flows along her head like fire.

Above them, the flight path of a plane. It moves across the sky, the hill, into prairie wind, and disappears.

The child's breaths cold on her face.

They both are smiling.

The man looks about this room he has painted the colour of evening sand. Things do not go together the way they come apart. Time props itself up like magazines in a cigar store; he is the browser. In the corner of his den he keeps an ancient globe, a map of the world the way it used to be, made up of simple elements: water, wind, earth, fire. Ancient history. He rubs his neck muscles which are always aching. History is no story with beginning, middle, end. It is a string of simultaneous events, past leaking into future; the future into past.

> *But the little prince was anxious. You were wrong to come. You'll suffer. I'll look as if I'm dead and that won't be true.*

The man's head commingles of late his many years of lessons. Radio waves have always existed; people just didn't have the ability to detect them. A rainbow doesn't exist as a material object. It appears in a different place to each observer.

The man looks out his darkening window. Nothing in the way of evidence — no letter, phone call, touch. Only a dog's dream to say that she was real. He feels his life repeated in a thousand empty lives. Energy slips in its entirety to another level, no longer made of particles; it exists, but it's a wave. The dark brings such sharp loneliness; the heart asking too much.

A flutter. The man turns in his dusky flaxen room. His dog rises, growling, on the far side of the wall. She pads down the hall paralleling the man's den. Growling softly, she seats herself outside the closed door. A flutter at his cheek. Butterfly-wing light. His hand rises to the touch. A moth? No. Quick and silver, he feels the fluted air, the strange world breathing.

> *Goodbye, said the fox. Here is my secret. It's quite*
> *simple. One sees clearly only with the heart.*
> *Anything essential is invisible to the eyes.*

The man looks out across the city, across the future, present, past, where stories come apart; where you catch sight in pieces.

Listen.

Melody floats the room
the settling ashes
pure, desiring
he cups her in his hands.

The child stands. Air fogs between them.

The prairie grasses sound a note.

Wind spills its gusts inside the woman.

Down below a light illuminates an upstairs room.

Night draws. It has begun to sprinkle. A storm gathering on the horizon.

The woman's veins rivers of molten glass. Air in the trees, the telephone wires sound A minor.

Allegro, cantabile, grazioso. Dolce.

The woman stops halfway down, looks back.

The child, darkening, merges with the landscape.

The note sounds clear now.

One beautiful still tone.

Umbilically corded.
Ne m'oublie pas.

The man sits in his den. He feels an energy. Late autumn sunlight floods his desk. The sun has long passed its summer solstice; the year is heading toward its shortest day. He holds a pen, looks through molecules of evening light. Einstein's Theory of Relativity has woven time and space together, curving through the stars, bending light away from a straight line. Several particles in a single quantum system share a single inseparable psi field: entangled. Erwin Schrödinger called entanglement the most profound characteristic of quantum mechanics. Einstein called it spooky. Anything that happens to one particle affects the other. They could be in separate galaxies, yet remain in a single quantum state. The man's hands reach for his books. The world turns beneath your feet; you learn to right yourself. You learn to keep on walking. You learn too late that questions need not be answered; rather, answers must be questioned. You learn to live with choices. You learn to live with loss. No point in longing for the light; too much light blinds. His son's last visit the man took him up Nose Hill. The boy ran and ran, tireless, until he reached a large stone where he sat, waiting.

Nothing ceases to exist, the man said, joining his son on the rock. Matter turns back to energy. The boy kicked his football, ran to retrieve it, wiggled back up beside the man. Did you know, the man said, that we are made of atoms formed from hydrogen in stars? That stars are most radiant when they die? We're made from stars that died long before our world was formed. We're made from stardust.

The man gets up, makes himself some tea. The recent many-worlds theory of quantum mechanics suggests that the world splits, creating multiple universes. Each one real. Time loses all meaning when you jump from world to world. For reasons physicists can't yet understand, people only see their own.

The man pulls down a mug from the top shelf. All you can do is seek to fulfill the mind's yearning. That's what physics is, a fairy tale, small glimpses of our world projecting us into a timeless universe where anything can happen. The bigger a scientist's imagination, the more possible events he can see. It is thinking that keeps the man from going crazy.

He carries his tea into the den. All around, the sound of light. He thinks of Galileo, born to the sound of his father's lute. Swept into this world on the music of the universe.

Tonight, the moon is tossed and low. The clouds skim by in fragments, whisk between the stars. The dog is agitated, snuffling. Once, the man longed for certainty, permanence. Those constructs do not exist. The only permanent discoveries are those of the imagination. He walks to the darkening window.

He thinks of the woman. Outside, the lonely signals of a late autumn storm. Lightning knifes the sky. The two of them moving past each other like the song of trains, heading in opposite directions, glimpsing through reflected glass, the glimmer, each other's light.

He breathes to sew his splintered chest together. He picks up his pen. He will tell his class about interference. How when two waves combine they interfere with each other. Then one of two things happens. They can add to each other to make a bigger wave. This cooperative action is called constructive interference.

But, if, by their combination, they cancel each other out, what's left is destructive interference.

Her words. His silence.

Then you can't get anywhere. You just go up and down, until you break the wave. The den in darkness. He moves to illumine a light.

If what we believe of quantum mechanics is true, every time we observe the universe, we disturb it.

Yet nothing meaningful happens until you entangle yourself.

A dead cat and a live one.

He looks at the silver-peppered sky and sees six thousand stars.

There is no official version.

A box. She holds in her arms a brief melody of child. *Da capo*. Repeat from the beginning. She turns from the Files Access Office and carries the evidence down the long corridor, steps into November wind. Weight in her arms. This terrible stack of charts, this record of a life. She envisions the papers scattering like ashes, crumbling, dust. She unlocks the car door, belts the cardboard box into the front seat. Leaves fling against the headlights. She drives. Wind fills her throat. She drives, imagining a future.

In the mudroom she kicks off her shoes, walks stocking-footed, silent through her sunlit kitchen. Wind gusts against the house.

He stands in his physics classroom, seeing a great distance. Listen.

He is with her on the lip of Nose Hill, overlooking Calgary's glass skyline, rushed wind, air skimming, scattered wild roses. He brushes a finger to the child's translucent skin.

The child's face in light. Tell me the story.

She lifts the lid
A trace of song
Scattering scars
The sough of a child
Once upon a time

A special thank you to:

The Markin-Flanagan Distinguished Writers Programme for affording me a prodigious year as Canadian writer-in-residence to pursue this manuscript while rubbing shoulders with Albertan, Canadian, and international writers.

The Banff Centre's five-week Writing Studio during which I put down the first words of *Kalila*.

The Leighton Artists' Colony, also at the Banff Centre, for repeated sojourns in the Hemingway and Evamy studios and for beauty and solitude in which to dream this story.

The International Retreat for Writers at Hawthornden Castle, Lasswade, Scotland, for insisting upon silence and allowing me five weeks to live inside the manuscript.

The University of Windsor, its English professors, students, and community, for so warmly welcoming me as writer-in-residence while I did final edits on *Kalila*.

The Canada Council for the Arts, the Alberta Foundation for the Arts, and the Woodcock Fund for their financial support.

***

This book has been influenced in different stages by talented, generous friends, each of whom offered his/her own unique contribution to *Kalila*. My deepest gratitude to my two equally fabulous long-time editors:

Nicole Markotić, who was on board long before this book's inception. Thank you for your legendary edits, for keeping me afloat through its numerous transformations, for slashing and chopping, for all those energizing Starbucks conversations, and the airport and errand runs so we could keep talking about what mattered. And to Margaret Markotić for accepting me as another daughter whenever Nicole is in town.

Suzette Mayr for your brilliant suggestions that shook this book into its present form, for your infectious enthusiasm, for your belief. For being my writing buddy, for practically sending the manuscript out for me when I got discouraged. And to you and Tonya, always, for your warm hospitality.

My deepest thanks also go to:

Bethany Gibson, Goose Lane's editor extraordinare, for *seeing Kalila*. For your exceptional first-class edits that came from head and heart combined. For your remarkable otherworldly wisdom. It was a transcendent experience for which I will never stop being grateful.

Aritha van Herk for graciously taking a draft with you to the North Pole one Christmas and writing that tough, terrific, six-page single-spaced critique instead of tobogganing.

Stan Dragland for kindly putting your busy life on hold to read and edit a draft and nudge me in the right direction.

Linda and Esta Spalding for reading and commenting on excerpts on the road to Banff in the old van.

Tom Dilworth for large-heartedly reading the manuscript in the midst of term's end and scribbling sharp, perfecting edits that made a marked difference to the final draft.

Julie Scriver for an exquisite cover and layout.

Angela Williams for your thoroughness in searching out permissions.

Gordon Drake, physicist, for your elegant equations.

Bob Nixon for your numerous physics talks and edits.

Karen Lean for your care, for standing up for her.

Karen Martin for sharing conversations and your Masters thesis, *When a Baby Dies of SIDS*, Qualitative Research Press, with me.

Various Deckert-Roth-Nixon family members for your medical and physics and hunting conversations, and Carol and David Roth for again offering your lovely snowy Fernie log house as a writing retreat.

My beautiful children, Jordan and Madeleine, whose love and presence sustain me, and your lovely partners, Kelsey Hough and Ryan Stewart, for being family through it all.

And last but not least, Julie, Akou, Susanne, Corey, Heather, and again, Bethany, for making everything about working with Goose Lane a remarkable experience.

Excerpts of *Kalila* have appeared in *Tesseract*, *Rampike*, *The New Quarterly*, *Intersections* (Banff Centre Press), and *Threshold* (University of Alberta Press).

The following authors and lyricists, to whom I owe a debt of gratitude, were cited by the characters in this novel.

p. 37 The lyrics are from "Leaning on the Everlasting Arms" by Elisha A. Hoffman and Anthony J. Showalter.

p. 38 "Close up the casement, shut out that stealing moon" comes from "Shut Out That Moon" by Thomas Hardy, which appeared in *The Norton Anthology of Modern Poetry*, edited by Richard Ellmann and Robert O'Clair (New York: W.W. Norton & Company, 1973).

p. 38 "You promised to buy me a bonny blue ribbon..." is excerpted from a traditional nursery rhyme, "Oh Dear, What Can the Matter Be?", which appeared in http://americanfolklore.net/folklore/2010/07/more_nursery_rhymes_about_peop.html

pp. 48 and 49 The lyrics are from "Under His Wings" by William D. Cushing and Ira D. Sankey.

pp. 58-59 The lyrics are from "Walk Right Back." Words and Music by Sonny Curtis. © 1960 (Renewed) Warner-Tamerlane Publishing Corp. All Rights Reserved.

p. 74 The lyrics are from "If I Didn't Care." Written by Jack Lawrence. Used by permission of Range Road Music, Inc. and © 1939 Chappell & Co., Inc. (ASCAP) All Rights Reserved.

p. 79 Excerpt from *The Little Prince* by Antoine de Saint-Exupéry, copyright 1943 and renewed 1971 by Harcourt, Inc. reprinted by permission of Houghton Mifflin Publishing Company.

p. 87 The lyrics are from "Mockin' Bird Hill" by Vaughn Horton. Used by permission of Peer Music.

p. 87 The lyrics are from "Way Up High in a Cherry Tree." Traditional song.

p. 102 The lyrics are from "Onward Christian Soldiers" by Sabine Baring-Gould and Arthur S. Sullivan.

p. 103 This excerpt is from "The Eolian Harp," Samuel Taylor Coleridge, *The Complete Poetical Works of Samuel Taylor Coleridge*, Vol. I & II, edited by Ernest Hartley Coleridge (London: Oxford, 1912).

p. 115 The lyrics are from "Baby's Bed's a Silver Moon" from *Lullabies: An Illustrated Songbook*, edited by Richard Kapp (New York: The Metropolitan Museum of Art, 1997).

p. 118 The lyrics are from "Sing Your Way Home." Traditional song.

pp. 130-131 Excerpt from *The Little Prince* by Antoine de Saint-Exupéry, copyright 1943 and renewed 1971 by Harcourt, Inc. reprinted by permission of Houghton Mifflin Publishing Company.

p. 134 Excerpt from Albert Einstein in a letter to the family of his friend Michele Besso (March 1955) from Freeman Dyson, *Disturbing the Universe* (New York: Harper & Row, 1979).

p. 171 The lyrics are from "Baby's Bed's a Silver Moon" from *Lullabies: An Illustrated Songbook*, edited by Richard Kapp (New York: The Metropolitan Museum of Art, 1997).

p. 175 Quotation from P.L. Travers, author of *Mary Poppins*, which appeared in "Personal View: Books," *Sunday Times,* December 11, 1988.

p. 181 The lyrics are from "Hush Little Baby." Traditional song.

pp. 186, 209-210, 233-234, 239, 240 Excerpts from *The Little Prince* by Antoine de Saint-Exupéry, copyright 1943 and renewed 1971 by Harcourt, Inc. reprinted by permission of Houghton Mifflin Publishing Company.

Rosemary Nixon penned *Kalila* on two continents over fifteen years. She is the author of two previous short story collections, *Mostly Country* and *The Cock's Egg*, winner of the Howard O'Hagan Short Fiction Award. Nixon has taught creative writing at the University of Calgary, Chinook College, and Sage Hill Writing Experience. She was Canadian Writer-in-Residence for the Markin-Flanagan Distinguished Writers Programme and at the University of Windsor.